GIRL
IN
THE
MIRROR

GIRL
IN
THE
MIRROR

BY ZOA SHERBURNE

William Morrow and Company
New York 1966

Fifth Printing

TO NORENE, WITH LOVE

GIRL
IN
THE
MIRROR

ONE

She waited, well hidden by the heavy curtains in the living room, and saw her father's car drive slowly down the tree-shaded avenue and park across the street from the apartment entrance.

They didn't get out of the car at once, so Ruth Ann had ample opportunity to study the enemy. Even this far away she could see that the woman was attractive. She wore a pink coat, which was probably very feminine and clever of her; everyone knew that older men liked pink.

Watching, Ruth Ann had the miserable feeling that she was walking through a nightmare—a nightmare that she had been lost in a hundred times . . . a thousand times. She had never admitted to herself that she was afraid her father might marry again. She had tried to ignore the possibility with the childish wishful thinking that if she didn't think about it, it would go away.

Ruth Ann looked away from the couple in the parked car and around at the apartment that was almost exactly the same as it had been when her mother had died four years before. The same pictures were on the wall, the same furniture grouped in the same position, even the curtains that had been replaced were almost identical duplicates of the ones her mother had selected. Friends had always assured them that Ruth Ann's mother, with her wonderful feeling for color and line and arrangement, could have been a professional decorator. But she hadn't been interested in a career; she'd been perfectly happy being a wife and a mother.

The couple across the street had left the car now and were walking up to the corner crossing. Another man might have crossed in the middle of the block, but not Ruth Ann's father. Even on a Sunday morning when there was no traffic to speak of he kept firmly to the letter of the law.

Ruth Ann stepped back into the center of the room, trying not to look at herself in the mirror over the mantle as she yanked at her shapeless dark skirt and tugged her blouse into a smoother line. She told herself, belatedly, that it had probably been a mistake to wear a blouse and skirt. They had a tendency to chop her in half and make her look even more enormous than usual. She didn't look quite so fat in a dress with straight lines but, on the other hand, the enemy might as well know the worst. Right from the first she might as well understand that no matter how attractive she found the man she would, in a sense, be marrying his glaringly unattractive daughter as well.

Ruth Ann was seated on the living-room sofa with the funny papers spread out around her when her father's key turned in the lock and they came in. She looked up and waited.

"Hi, honey," her father said. "This is Tracy."

Tracy. She couldn't even have a sensible woman-like name. Tracy sounded like . . . like a cartoon character.

Ruth Ann got to her feet awkwardly. She did everything awkwardly. "Hello," she said flatly. Not, I'm-pleased-to-meet-you or how-do-you-do or any of the pleasant meaningless greetings. Why should she pretend? Why should she be a hypocrite?

Tracy Emery regarded her unsmilingly. "Hello, Ruth," she said. "I hope you don't mind if I call you Ruth instead of Ruth Ann."

"Why should I mind?" Ruth Ann said, as if she couldn't care less. "I'm called a lot of things. One of my best friends calls me Porky."

She could see that her father was disturbed at the turn the conversation was taking, but Tracy Emery shrugged it off. "I still think I'll call you Ruth," she said mildly.

Her father was helping the enemy off with her coat, and Ruth Ann saw that her dress was the same

13

luscious shade of pink. It was a linenlike sheath and so simple that it must have cost a great deal of money. She wasn't wearing any jewelry except a plain gold cross suspended on a fine chain.

Close up she didn't look as young as she had at first glance. There was even a touch of gray in her dark hair, but her eyes were warm and interested, and she moved lightly like a ballet dancer as she crossed the room and settled in a chair by the window.

"It's a beautiful room," she said, ignoring Ruth Ann and speaking to Mr. Callahan. "Exactly right."

"I'm glad," he said, as if he might have been harboring some doubts about the rightness of the room and her words had dispelled them. He looked at Ruth Ann, who was still standing in the midst of the clutter of newspapers, then. "How about rustling us up some lemonade, honey?"

It sounded almost as if he were trying to get rid of her. She went past him wordlessly and into the kitchen, blinking hard to hold back the unexpected tears that stung behind her lashes. She could hear them talking as she got the lemonade from the freezing compartment, diluted it with water, and filled the company glasses with chipped ice and a maraschino cherry. It was going to be worse than she had feared, much worse. The enemy wasn't going to fight back, not by a word or gesture or disapproving

14

glance. But then why should she fight? She probably considered the battle won.

Ruth went back into the living room with the three tall glasses balanced on a tray. The enemy was standing beside the spinet piano, running her fingers lightly over the keys. She looked up with a quick smile. "The room was designed to fit around the piano, wasn't it?"

Ruth put the tray down on the coffee table. She didn't even bother to look up. "It was my mother's piano. She decorated the apartment herself."

"I know," Tracy said, as if she really did know and didn't mind in the least. "It always shows when someone designs a room for love instead of money. You usually see the money, but you can feel the love."

Ruth Ann did look up then, and she hoped her eyes weren't as mutinous as her thoughts. *Does she really think she can win me over with obvious remarks like that? Is she so stupid that she thinks it will make me* like *her?* But Tracy, as she accepted the glass of lemonade Ruth Ann offered, didn't look stupid. She looked thoughtful and a little sorry, but certainly not stupid.

"I've been telling Tracy about our record collection," her father said, as he came over to pick up his glass. "Maybe she'd like to hear some of our favorites."

15

"Do we have to listen to records?" Ruth Ann knew that she sounded petulant and ungracious. "I mean . . . I'd planned on watching the midday movie, but of course if you'd rather not. . . ."

It was the blackest kind of treason. Her father knew perfectly well that she didn't especially care for television movies, and he had always maintained that it was rude to turn on television when guests were present unless they specifically requested it. But when Ruth Ann looked at her father, his eyes were carefully blank. Quite clearly he had no intention of starting a discussion today. Maybe he was sorry for her. Maybe both of them were sorry for her. She could imagine Tracy Emery and her father talking about her. Her father had probably explained that Ruth had this . . . well, this weight problem, and that was why she was shy about meeting new people, why she didn't care about going out with young people her own age. And of course Tracy, being a nurse, would know all about such things. She'd think that Ruth Ann's problem was *psychological*. Ruth Ann was beginning to hate that word.

"Very well, honey," her father said now. "Go ahead and watch your cowboy show. I'll take Tracy on the sixty-four-dollar personally conducted tour."

There was nothing to do except turn on the TV and pretend to be engrossed in the dull Western that was showing, while her father showed Tracy around the apartment and finally out into the kitchen where

16

they seemed to be having a fine time starting dinner preparations.

Sunday dinner was always Ruth Ann's responsibility. During the week, when she was going to school, Mrs. Malcome planned and prepared the meals so that Ruth Ann only had to turn on the oven and set the table after she got home at three thirty or four. But Sunday was her chance to shine in the culinary department. Her father was always bragging about what a good cook she was and suggesting that he had to spend so much time in the gym because of her. He was careful, though, not to point out that if she wasn't such a good cook she might not be so fat.

Her father never called her fat. Mrs. Malcome, who was normally the kindest person on earth, was sometimes a little acid about what she called "the child's weight problem."

"The trouble with you, Missy," she scolded Ruth from time to time, "is that eating is still your favorite indoor sport. It's fine that you're such a good cook, but do you have to be your own best customer?"

It was easy for Ruth Ann to tell herself that Mrs. Malcome might be a little jealous. Mrs. Malcome cooked plain foods; her cakes were edible, but not the poems that Ruth Ann could coax from the same recipe. Ruth Ann's pies were flaky and tender and she invented heavenly casseroles. She was, Mrs. Malcome admitted grudgingly, a born cook.

But Mrs. Malcome was always after her to look

17

outside herself for other interests—to take up skating or swimming or ballet. She said that Ruth Ann should learn to burn up those extra calories, but the trouble was that the more she exercised the hungrier she got and the more she ate. It was a vicious circle.

I'll bet Tracy Emery is a terrible cook, Ruth Ann told herself, as she slumped in front of the television set. I'll bet she doesn't know how to boil water.

It seemed hours before the miserable movie was over and she could go out into the kitchen. Tracy had already taken charge. Ruth Ann's father was cutting vegetables for a salad and he seemed to be enjoying himself. He was wearing the patio apron that had been purchased with an eye to their building a place on their country property with an outdoor barbecue and a flower garden and all the other little touches of country living. The dream, however, had died along with Ruth's mother.

Tracy was sliding the lamb chops under the broiler.

"Your timing is just about perfect," Ruth Ann's father greeted her. "We'll be ready to sit down in about fifteen minutes. How about setting the table?"

"In the dining alcove?" she asked woodenly.

His eyebrows shot up. "Naturally in the dining alcove," he said. "Would we expect our guest to eat in the kitchen?"

She gave him a long look, but he had already turned his attention back to the salad.

It would probably be an atrocious salad, she reminded herself as she put the best china on the place mats and started dealing out the silverware. Her father was simply out of his element in a kitchen. He didn't even know that vegetable greens should be torn into bite-size pieces instead of whacked at with a knife. And the lamb chops would be ruined. Both Ruth Ann and her father liked them fried until the fat was golden brown and crispy.

She went back to the kitchen when the table was ready and asked if there was anything else she could do.

Tracy Emery was sprinkling vinegar into the salad bowl, but she looked up long enough to give Ruth Ann a smile. "I think we have everything under control. The asparagus is just about ready."

Ruth Ann glanced at the stove. "No sauce?" she asked politely. "Dad likes cheese sauce with his asparagus."

"No sauce," Tracy said brightly. "No potatoes either. He really doesn't need all that starch."

Ruth Ann felt her cheeks burn. Tracy might as well have added, And neither do you.

At the table she was quiet and kept her eyes on her plate. She didn't enjoy the dinner the way she normally enjoyed her meals. It seemed to lack seasoning

19

or imagination or something. But if her father and Tracy noticed that she wasn't eating much, neither of them commented.

Her father asked a lot of questions about the city hospital staff. He had spent some time in it last year, undergoing a series of tests for stomach ulcers, and there he had met Tracy. She had been one of the technical nurses, and he had seemed to like her a lot. He'd talked about her when he was home again, but Ruth Ann hadn't been smart enough to recognize the danger signals, or maybe she hadn't wanted to recognize them.

She had just been glad that he had found a friend, someone to run in and visit with him when he wanted visitors. It was hard for her to spend much time at the hospital because of her schoolwork and because there was no one available to drive her back and forth. Mrs. Malcome had stayed at the apartment with her, and she had managed to get in during the evening visiting hours, but that was all. Mr. Callahan was in the hospital almost three weeks, but when he was home again he was different. It wasn't just that he felt better, it was as if he had reached inside himself and found another person, one who wanted to live, not in the tranquil past but in the hazardous future.

Ruth Ann glanced at the woman across the table and found herself wondering why a man, an intelligent worldly man like her father, should find Tracy Emery so attractive. She certainly wasn't beautiful; she wasn't even pretty, in the soft feminine way that Ruth Ann's mother had been pretty. Tracy was slim and clear-eyed and she had white teeth and a nice smile, but there was nothing spectacular about her. She had smooth dark brown hair touched lightly with gray, and her nose was just an ordinary nose. If she had been young Ruth could understand it, but she was probably pushing forty.

Ruth Ann knew that her father was forty-four, but her mother had been a lot younger. He used to laugh and call her his child bride when he wanted to tease her. She'd been just past seventeen when he married her, and when she was thirty she died.

Ruth Ann's throat felt tight thinking about her mother. She hadn't really thought about her, or missed her, in months.

It was a relief when the telephone rang and she could push back her chair, mumble "excuse me," and escape to the small entry hall that was out of sight from the dining alcove.

It was Jeanie, just as Ruth Ann had known it would be, calling her.

"Did she come?" Jeanie asked at once. "Is she there now? Have they . . . you know . . . have they *said* anything yet?"

Ruth Ann felt a surge of annoyance. It really

wasn't any of Jeanie's business except . . . except that Ruth Ann had made it her business by talking about it so much. "Yes. We're having dinner, Jeanie. I'll call you back. O.K.?"

"But have they *said* anything?" Jeanie protested. "You can at least say yes or no, can't you?"

"I'll call you back as soon as I can," Ruth Ann said smoothly, and replaced the receiver while Jeanie was still sputtering.

She went back to the table and both her father and the enemy looked at her expectantly. "It wasn't important," she said. "Just a girl from school wanting to talk. I can call her back later."

There was no dessert—not even orange sherbet although there was a quart of it in the freezing compartment. Ruth Ann's father loved dessert and usually saved room for two pieces of cake or pie but, she hadn't felt like baking after he had announced that he was bringing Tracy Emery home for dinner.

"You don't mind if we leave you with the dishes, do you, honey?" her father asked, when they had finished their coffee. "Tracy has to be back at work this evening. She goes on duty at seven, but I promised to drive her out to see the country estate this afternoon."

Ruth Ann looked down at her plate. "I don't mind doing the dishes," she said.

No one asked if she wanted to go. No one bothered

to find out how she felt about having her father take a stranger out to a place that had been part of an old dream. It had been months since her father had offered to drive her out to the country estate, which was the ridiculous title they had given the acre tract that would someday be the site of their dream house.

Several times since her mother died real-estate agents had approached her father about buying the property, but Ruth Ann's father didn't want to let it go. She told herself that it was because the three of them had been so happy planning the home that would someday top the little rise of ground looking out across the valley. It would be like selling your happiest memories. There were even some house plans—very amateurish—that they had slaved over. They had marked off the rooms to scale, and then changed the rooms over and over, adding a porch here and an extra closet there. She remembered her father suggesting that it was much easier to change plans on paper, and certainly a lot cheaper.

But how awful if another woman were to move in and see all the plans brought to life. Because Tracy Emery couldn't possibly fit into the dream; she didn't belong.

"Thank you for letting me come to dinner," Tracy said at the door, as if the invitation had come from Ruth Ann, as if she had been consulted in the matter.

Ruth knew she ought to say something pleasant

about it having been a pleasure, but, on the other hand, why should she pretend? "I don't know why you should thank me," she said instead, "you did all the work."

Her father didn't kiss her good-by or even say anything to her as he followed Tracy out of the apartment, but she recognized the disapproval in his silence and she knew, with a sinking heart, that he was disappointed in her.

It hurt to know that he was disappointed, but she couldn't be really sorry. She told herself that she'd do it again, if necessary. After all, a woman who was planning to marry a man with another responsibility. . . .

But all her logic didn't excuse her behavior, and she knew it. Besides acting like a sulky child she had deliberately set out to give Tracy the worst possible impression. She could have fixed herself up and tried not to look like such a frump. She could have made the effort to be friendly, to talk to Tracy and make her feel welcome. She could have. . . .

Ruth Ann hurried through the dishes, and then whipped up a batch of brownies and put them in the oven. Her father loved having brownies to munch when he watched television. She folded all the newspapers and straightened the front room and dining room, pushing open the windows so that the food odors wouldn't linger. She piled all his favorite

24

records on the stereo and turned it low, so that the apartment would be filled with the sort of music he loved when he walked in.

It was frightening to think that he might be really angry with her, because that would mean that Tracy was as important as she feared. She glanced at the clock, and then went out to take the brownies from the oven. She was hungry again, but she always was when she hadn't eaten dessert.

The kitchen clock said it was only a little after five. Her father hadn't said he'd be right back after leaving Tracy at the hospital. Perhaps he'd go in and talk to some of the other staff members. Right this minute they were probably walking around the country estate. Was he showing her the view and pointing out where the dining room would open onto the patio? Would Tracy notice the twin cedars that seemed to be waiting for a curving driveway to cut between them? Or were they driving in the car and talking?

". . . have they said anything yet?" She seemed to hear the echo of Jeanie's excited whisper. Jeanie meant, Have they told you they plan to be married?

Right now, this very minute, they could be talking about it, talking about her. Ruth Ann was at least smart enough to know that she was the problem. She was the one her father would have to consider if he made up his mind to marry again. And what about Tracy? How would she feel about having a fat un-

25

gracious stepdaughter who clearly resented her? How would she feel about giving up her well-ordered existence to share a home with a man, however attractive he was, who was burdened with a daughter who would probably be on their hands for the rest of their life. Other girls grew up and married or found a job, but who would hire a girl like her? What fellow in his right mind would ever want to marry her?

Ruth Ann shrugged off the self-pitying notion and mixed a thin icing for the brownies. They tasted a lot better when they were iced.

I'll bet father's starved, too, she told herself, as she bit into one of the still-warm cookies. No potatoes, no sauce, no dessert. And she probably cut most of the fat off the lamb chops. That's the trouble with these naturally thin people; they never stop to think that other people might have different requirements.

She had three or four brownies, and then she went in to call Jeanie. They talked for a long, long time until one of Jeanie's sisters started having a fit because she wanted to use the phone.

"I have to hang up now," Jeanie said wearily. "You-know-who is having a tantrum. I'll see you at school tomorrow, and you can tell me all about it."

Ruth Ann hung up the phone with the feeling that Jeanie had been perfectly happy to surrender, that maybe Jeanie was a little tired of hearing her go on and on and on about Tracy Emery. She didn't expect

Jeanie to be as upset as she was over this unexpected turn of events, but she could at least pretend to sympathize. After all, Jeanie was her best friend.

They were together every day, walking to school and home again, sharing school lunches, trying hard to get into all the same classes. They did their homework together and went to the movies and school games as a twosome. The thing that had originally made them gravitate toward each other was that they both were fat. Jeanie weighed almost as much as Ruth Ann, although she was half a head shorter. They kidded about it and tried to pretend that they didn't mind, but it stung a little when they were mentioned in the school paper as Chubby and Tubby. One of the girls, who probably thought of herself as terribly funny, had dubbed them the King-Size Bookends. What really bothered Ruth Ann, though, was when her classmates or teachers called her Jeanie. Except for being overweight they didn't look anything alike. Ruth Ann had light brown hair that curled up on the ends and dark blue eyes and thick stubby lashes. Jeanie was dark and her hair was straight as a string. She was always complaining because her mother wouldn't let her get a permanent until she took off fifteen pounds.

Privately Ruth Ann felt that she carried her weight a great deal more gracefully than Jeanie, who was barely five foot two. But then Jeanie probably

27

thought of herself as a much smaller girl than Ruth Ann, who was almost four inches taller.

When nosey people like Mrs. Malcome came right out and asked how much she weighed, Ruth Ann usually said she wasn't sure, that she hadn't been on the scales lately. "I think around a hundred and sixty-two or three," she'd murmur, knowing perfectly well that it was over a hundred and eighty.

Sometimes she dreamed of stepping on the scales and finding that the arrow only went up to a hundred and fifteen pounds. A few times she'd even made herself go on a real crash diet. She'd practically starved herself for three days, and then gained back all the weight she lost during the following week. The school nurse had given her a diet to follow and even suggested she have their family doctor check her over and prescribe some pills, but Ruth Ann hadn't wanted to bother her father with such foolishness. Her father might think she was sick, and what would be the use of worrying him?

She heard her father's key in the lock while she was still sitting in the dark listening to the stereo music. Without glancing at the clock, she knew that it was after nine. She'd been listening to the clock chime the hour and then the half hour ever since seven o'clock.

Her father came in and hung away his jacket without bothering to click on the light. He turned on the table lamp, though, just before he sat down in his big comfortable chair and put his head back against the cushion as if he were suddenly very tired.

"You didn't like Tracy, did you?" he asked. But he was making a statement not asking a question.

"I . . . I haven't thought about it one way or another," Ruth Ann said, not quite truthfully. "I don't even know her."

"You'll have plenty of opportunity to know her," he said. "I've asked Tracy to marry me, and she's promised to think it over." When Ruth Ann said nothing, he looked across at her gravely. "Does the idea displease you?"

She swallowed, but she was proud of her voice when it finally emerged. "If it's what will make you happy, Father. . . ."

"It will make me happy," he assured her. "But we want to know how you feel about it. How will you feel about having a new mother?"

"She wouldn't be my mother," Ruth Ann reminded him. "I remember my mother."

There was a silence before he answered. "I remember her, too, Ruthy." He hadn't called her Ruthy for a long time, not for years, and he didn't seem to notice that he had used the name now.

After a moment he got up, switched off the record player, and found a program he liked on television. He wasn't going to say anything more about Tracy Emery, at least not tonight.

"I made some brownies," Ruth Ann said during

the first commercial. "They turned out pretty well. Can I bring you some?"

He thought for a moment, and then patted his stomach regretfully. "I guess not, honey. Tracy's right about that. I really don't need all those extra calories."

Before going to bed Ruth Ann went into the kitchen and put the brownies into a cookie jar. It was a temptation to slip a couple of them in her pocket for a bedtime snack, but she sternly resisted the impulse. For some reason she kept seeing Tracy in her slim pink sheath.

She went back into the living room and kissed her father good-night.

"G'night, honey," he said, without taking his eyes from the television screen, "I'll see you in the morning."

TWO

Ruth Ann told Jeanie all about her horrible Sunday as they walked to school the next day. She explained in detail everything Tracy had said, the clothes she wore, the way she looked. It was funny how she could remember almost word-for-word the remarks that Tracy had made about the apartment.

They went on to their classes, and then Ruth Ann started all over again when they sat down to lunch in the school cafeteria. She told her about the plain gold cross that Tracy wore on a thin chain—no earrings or rings or even a wristwatch, just the cross.

After a while she could see that Jeanie's attention was wandering. She just wasn't that interested in Ruth Ann's problem. Ruth stopped abruptly in the middle of a long monologue about the unimaginative meal Tracy had prepared, and the other girl sighed with what could only be relief.

"Well anyway, Ruth Ann," she said with determined cheerfulness, "now you don't have to be cooped up in that apartment all alone while your father is working. You'll have someone to talk to and watch television with. You might even get to like her if you give her a chance."

Ruth Ann looked at her friend coldly. "It's easy enough for you to look on the bright side of things. It doesn't matter to you one way or another."

Jeanie looked offended. "I was only saying that if you didn't go out of your way to look at the *grim* side of everything, you might not be so upset about this. Why, Ruth Ann, I know girls who are crazy about their stepmothers."

"Name three," Ruth Ann said.

"Besides, it could be a lot worse," Jeanie reminded her. "What if he married someone with three or four children like Helen's father did? You'd be a built-in baby-sitter and never have a minute to yourself."

Ruth Ann finished her sandwich and folded her paper napkin instead of crumpling it up. She got to her feet and spoke in a calm distant voice. "If you have finished eating, we'd better get started back before the bell rings."

Jeanie scrambled up to follow, her round flushed face mirroring her distress. "I just said that things could be worse," she muttered. "After all, it isn't as if you're a child. In a couple of years you'll be old enough to leave home if you don't get along with your father's new wife."

Ruth Ann refrained from pointing out that she

didn't *want* to leave home, she couldn't leave home. Her father was the most important person in her entire world, the *only* important person in her world. She had expected to be taking care of him forever and ever. Right now, while she was still in school, it was hard; but later there would be nothing to do but look after his comforts, plan the meals he enjoyed, keep the apartment clean and his clothes in order. They would be even closer companions when she was older; he'd talk to her about his work and the people he met. They liked the same things and laughed at the same jokes, and her father's eyes were filled with love whenever he looked at her. She knew he didn't see a fat rather ordinary-looking girl with a dull personality . . . he saw . . . he saw. . . .

Ruth Ann was glad when the bell rang and she could hurry away from Jeanie's determined cheerfulness. She was so glad to make her escape that she didn't watch where she was going and she ran headlong into a boy who was coming out of the chemistry lab. He made a grunting, wounded sound as he bent to retrieve his notebook. "Hey, watch it Fatso," he murmured, as he straightened up. And then something—maybe the sudden hurt that flooded Ruth Ann's eyes, or the fact that he was a well-mannered boy who just didn't think before he spoke, or something—made him duck his head and grin and say, "S'cuse me. It was my fault, Ruth Ann."

33

She went on toward her first afternoon class feeling more miserable than ever. Ruth Ann knew who *he* was, of course. Everyone in the school knew Tony Barretto. But she hadn't dreamed that he knew her name.

Tony was a junior this year, in Ruth Ann's class, although he was seventeen, a year older. He was just about the most popular boy in the entire school. Everyone yelled, "Hi, Tony," or "How goes it, boy?" or something friendly when they passed him in the halls. It was strange, too, because there wasn't anything outstanding about Tony. He wasn't good in sports and he didn't drive a souped-up car. According to word-of-mouth reports from those girls who had been lucky enough to date him, he wasn't even a good dancer. But he was so *nice*. He went out of his way to be nice to people—even people like Miss Hodges, who was so mean that she flunked people just for the fun of it. He joked with her and jumped to hold the door and help her with her coat and things like that—things the better-looking boys never bothered about. The class would probably make him an officer next year and vote him the boy most likely to succeed in its prophecy.

Ruth Ann mentioned Tony to Jeanie when they were walking home that afternoon. She had sense enough to keep away from the subject of Tracy Emery, and he seemed like a safe enough topic. "I ran into Tony Barretto this afternoon," she said, casually and with absolute truth. "And I got to thinking. Do you think I should call myself Ruth instead of Ruth Ann?"

Jeanie looked at her owl-eyed. "What has that to do with Tony Barretto, for goodness sakes?"

"Well . . . nothing really. Except that when he said Ruth Ann. . . ." She paused and shrugged. "I don't know. All of a sudden it struck me that Ruth Ann sounds sort of juvenile."

Jeanie was regarding her suspiciously. "I didn't know he even knew your name," she said with unflattering candor. "What were you two talking about?"

"Oh, Tony knows everyone's name. Haven't you noticed?" She ignored the last question. "I think that's probably why he's so popular. He cares about remembering names and things like that."

Jeanie's eyes started to dance. "Why Ruth Ann Callahan," she said softly, "you have a *crush* on Tony Barretto!"

"I don't have a crush on him, silly. I just said. . . ."

"You're blushing," Jeanie crowed. "You are too, blushing. . . ."

"I think you're out of your *tree*," Ruth Ann said crossly. "How silly can you get, for heaven's sake?" But she hastened her steps a little and she could feel that her ears were burning.

Jeanie plodded along at her heels, like a faithful

35

out-of-breath shadow, but just before they reached the malt shop she gave up and wheezed to a halt. "What are we running for?" she gasped. "Are we supposed to be in a race or something?"

Ruth Ann stopped. "I'm sorry, Jeanie." There was vague satisfaction in knowing that at least she wasn't as winded as Jeanie was. Her heart was thumping, but she wasn't gasping like a fish out of water. "I'm in sort of a hurry to get home. I've got to take the hem up on a couple of skirts."

"You mean you don't want to stop for a milk shake?" Jeanie asked. "It's my treat this Monday."

Ruth Ann hesitated. On Monday they practically always stopped for a milk shake. It had become as routine as brushing their teeth. As routine as sorting out the laundry and putting it away on Wednesday and making out the market list on Friday and. . . .

But even though she could *see* how the milk shake would look—pale brown and swirley in the frosted glass—and even though her mouth watered recalling that first long delicious sip through the straw, something made her hesitate. She could hear a couple of voices. A woman's voice, a light casual voice saying, "He doesn't need all that starch, and neither do you." And then another voice, Tony's voice, "Hey, watch it, Fatso."

"I guess I'll skip it this afternoon, Jeanie," she heard herself say. "I don't seem to be very hungry, and anyway I should get started on those skirts and my homework. Dad's taking me to the movies tonight."

"Lucky you," Jeanie said. "My father hates the movies, except those free ones on television. He says there's no sense spending all that money on first runs when we can wait a few years and see the same movies on the late, late show. Of course, Mother says that it's because he won't make the effort to get dressed up and go out. She says that someday she's going to divorce him and name that idiot box as corespondent."

Ruth Ann's smile felt a little stiff. She had heard all this twenty or thirty times. Jeanie had a habit of repeating and repeating herself. "I really do have to run," she broke in finally. "See you in the morning. O.K.?"

She patted her friend's arm before she moved on. Jeanie would probably hate going into the malt shop by herself. She didn't know many of the other girls well enough to sit with them, and she would feel conspicuous sitting on one of those stools at the counter.

I wonder if I bore Jeanie as much as she bores me sometimes, Ruth Ann thought, as she hurried toward the apartment building. We've known each other too long and spent too much time together—that's our problem. Why I can almost tell what Jeanie's going to say the moment she opens her mouth, and she probably can do the same for me. It's worse than being *married* to someone.

When Ruth Ann reached the apartment she thought about walking up the three flights of stairs instead of waiting for the elevator. But then she remembered that she'd read an article somewhere stating it was bad for overweight people to climb a lot of stairs. Climbing overtaxed their hearts or something.

Glad that no one else was waiting, she got into the self-service elevator and jabbed the button for the third floor. It was such a small elevator that she always felt she was taking up most of the room and that other people were grinning about it, or trying not to grin, which was just as bad.

When she let herself into the apartment, the telephone was ringing. "Hello, Ruth Ann," her father said, when she answered. "What's on the menu tonight?"

"I thought we might have hamburgers," Ruth Ann said, "with cheese and sweet pickles and lettuce and tomato. I'll make a yummy dessert and then, if we stack the dishes, we can make the first show."

"That's what I was calling about," her father said. "I thought it might be a good idea to invite Tracy to join us. She says she hasn't been to a good movie in months."

"Oh," Ruth Ann said, and hoped that she didn't sound as disappointed as she felt at the moment. "I'm not sure we have enough ground meat, but I can always run out and get some more."

"No problem," her father assured her easily. "We can skip the hamburgers and go to dinner after the movie. How does that strike you?"

"What . . . what time shall I be ready?" she asked.

"That's another thing." He sounded rushed, as if someone had come into the office and he was trying to get away from her. "Why don't you get on the bus and come down here? I have some extra work I'd like to clear away, and I could meet you and Tracy in the lobby around six thirty. O.K.?"

"O.K." she echoed tonelessly.

"And you'd better grab yourself a sandwich to tide you over," he reminded her. "We'll be eating fashionably late."

She hung up the phone and then stood glowering at it, as if it were somehow the telephone's fault. *Grab yourself a sandwich*—as if she were about six years old! She couldn't remotely imagine his advising Tracy to grab herself a sandwich because they'd be eating late.

Still scowling, she went into her room and opened the closet door, trying to decide what she should wear. She had some really good clothes, from the best shops in town, but nothing she put on looked smart. The suits that were darling in size eight or ten always looked like potato sacks when Ruth Ann wore them. All of her dresses were dark and cut in simple lines that were supposed to minimize her girth. She and Jeanie read all the magazine articles about big girls and how they could "dress down" their size. It sounded easy, the way the magazines described it, and some of the overweight girls used to illustrate the articles managed to look trim and smart. The trouble was that those girls, even though they weighed as much as Ruth Ann, had their weight distributed in more interesting places. And they were *tall*. Everyone knew that tall girls could carry their weight with no difficulty.

Ruth Ann had tried all the advice the magazines gave—stand-tall and tuck-in-your-rear. She had even invested in a couple of good girdles, although she hated them because they made her feel like an oversize sausage bulging at both ends, but nothing really helped. "Let's face it," she told her mirrored image, "you're just a slob."

Finally she selected a navy blue dress with touches of white here and there. The salesgirl had insisted that it really *did* things for Ruth, but what she probably meant was that a navy blue circus tent was less conspicuous than one in a lighter color.

Her head was beginning to ache by the time she had half finished dressing. The more she thought about walking into a restaurant with her father and Tracy Emery, the worse she felt. Slowly she went into the living room and called her father. She told him that she had a splitting headache, and if he didn't mind she'd skip the dinner and movie.

He sounded quite upset. "Ruth Ann, do you really have a headache? This isn't another childish effort to snub Tracy, is it?"

"Of course not," she said quickly, too quickly. "I really feel awful. Maybe I'm coming down with something."

"Did you take one of your pills?" he asked. "That usually helps the headaches."

She crossed her fingers behind her back. "Of course I remembered the pills, but maybe they haven't had a chance to take effect yet."

"Maybe so," he said, still unconvinced. "Anyway, if you feel better in a little while you can come along. Tracy is stopping by for you. I was just about to call you when the phone rang. She said it was silly for you to take the bus when the apartment is right on her way. She'll probably be there within the hour."

"I'd better call her back and tell her I'm not feeling well," Ruth Ann said. "I'd hate to have her come all this way for nothing."

"She doesn't mind," he assured her. "The suggestion came from Tracy, not me. Anyway, you can't reach her at her place. She was just leaving when she

41

called me, because she had a couple of other stops to make."

When her father had rung off, Ruth Ann went out to the kitchen and took one of the pills her doctor had recommended. Her fib seemed a little less like a lie now.

For headaches or stomach distress, it said on the bottle. One every four hours. Probably nothing but aspirin, Ruth Ann told herself bleakly. The doctor didn't have much faith in her headaches. He'd asked her a lot of questions and talked to her about making a *game* of losing weight. Losing a pound a week —just one pound—and penalizing herself when she went over or under. She knew perfectly well what the doctor was thinking. He didn't believe she had headaches; he thought they were an excuse to get her out of doing the things she didn't want to do, such as helping to wait on table at the annual church breakfast, going to camp with the CYO group, trying out for the school orchestra. But Dr. Melburn was a skinny nervous little man, who probably ate like a bird. What did he know about anything? Why would he care if everyone at the church breakfast stared at her and asked who the fat girl was? Or if the girls at camp regarded her as a freak? Even playing the piano—her one real accomplishment—wouldn't make up for the ordeal of having to be the focus of so many curious eyes. What did Dr. Melburn know about being a misfit, a teen-age monstrosity?

Ruth Ann made herself a salami sandwich and munched on it drearily. She didn't really like salami, but her father was crazy about it. What she really liked was liverwurst. Still, everyone knew that liverwurst was loaded with calories.

She went back to her room and made herself lie quietly on the bed for a while, waiting for the pill to take effect. She kept hearing the disappointment in her father's voice. He didn't think she had a headache this time. Maybe he always believed that she made up the headaches to win his sympathy or to get out of doing something disagreeable.

After a while Ruth Ann got up and finished dressing. She put on a plastic bib and fussed with her hair for a long time until her arms got tired and she had to rest. Everyone said that she really had nice hair. Jeanie always complained because Ruth Ann's hair was naturally curly and her own dark mop was straight as a string.

The girl in the mirror looked back at Ruth Ann gravely. Sometimes that girl was almost pretty; if the light was just right and her head was tilted at just the right angle. At those times Ruth Ann could half-close her eyes and see the way she might look if she lost some weight. If she could lose forty or fifty pounds, she might not be so bad. Her skin was good, and she had dark blue eyes, light brown hair, and finely arched brows. Her mother's coloring had been the same, but her mother had been tiny. Why, Ruth Ann

43

had been taller and had outweighed her mother by ten pounds when she was eleven years old!

I could go on another diet, she told herself, pulling her stomach in and looking at her profile view. Not that it ever does much good.

Ruth Ann remembered her last diet all too well. Mrs. Malcome had set it up. For a week she had fed her pineapple and cottage cheese salads and nonfat milk and lean meats. She had packed Ruth Ann's lunch with two thin slices of diet bread, cheese, and the inevitable tomato. No butter or mayonnaise, no dessert unless one counted the orange or apple. For after school snacks she had celery and carrot sticks and boiled eggs served without salt. Offhand Ruth Ann could think of nothing less palatable than an egg without salt, but Mrs. Malcome said salt retained body fluid. Mrs. Malcome knew all about diets and talked about them by the hour. She was a chubby little woman, herself, and she went on the diet when Ruth Ann did, because she said it would be more fun if they could lose weight together. Ruth Ann had a suspicion that Mrs. Malcome cheated on her diet during the day or when she was at her own home.

Ruth Ann almost starved for five days. Finally she gave up and fortified herself with milk shakes and candy bars on her way to and from school. Of course, she never mentioned these extras to Mrs. Malcome, and Mrs. Malcome, who probably had a guilty conscience herself, never asked. She finally decided that Ruth Ann's fat must be glandular. "She ate like a bird for an entire week," she heard Mrs. Malcome confiding to someone over the phone. "I even packed her lunch so she wouldn't be tempted by all those fattening foods in the school cafeteria. But she only lost about a pound."

The doorbell sounded and Ruth Ann took off the plastic bib before she went out to admit Tracy Emery.

Tracy smiled as if they were on the best of terms. "Good afternoon," she said gaily. "I came to give you a lift downtown. Did your father get in touch with you?"

She looked so slim and smart that Ruth could have cried. "I'm not quite ready," she said. "Won't you come in?"

Tracy came in and tossed her fur cape across the end of the davenport. Her suit was slim and brown, her shoes had high heels that matched her purse, and her gloves picked up the color of the scarf tucked inside her suit jacket. Ruth Ann had a vision of herself waddling into a restaurant in her dowdy navy blue. It was only reasonable to believe that her father liked to be seen with someone attractive, someone he could be proud of. He was just being polite when he suggested that Ruth Ann come with them.

"When you're ready," Tracy said, "I thought we

might take a little drive before meeting your father. We seem to have a great deal to talk about."

It was probably like her to be so direct, Ruth Ann thought bitterly. She was certainly cutting off any hope of a graceful retreat.

"I called Father and told him that I had a terrible headache," she said. "But it was too late to reach you."

"Oh?" Tracy said, and waited.

She knows my headache wasn't that bad; she knows I was making excuses because I didn't want to go. Aloud she said, "I took one of my pills, though, and now my headache seems much better."

"That's good," Tracy said. "A drive in the fresh air may be just what you've been needing."

Ruth Ann got her coat. At least in it she was reasonably camouflaged. She followed Tracy out of the building and across the street to where her car was parked. It was a good car—special nurses probably made a great deal of money. Ruth Ann studied Tracy as she got behind the wheel and eased the car out into the traffic.

"I hope you aren't nervous with a woman driver," Tracy said without looking directly at Ruth. "I've only been driving for a couple of years, and I guess it's hard for an older person to have the confidence you youngsters seem to be born with."

Ruth resisted asking why she had waited so long— well, she had to be past thirty-five—before learning to drive. If Tracy wanted her to know she would tell her.

They hadn't turned toward the freeway that would take them into town. Instead, Tracy drove out to a residential section that was still under construction. Here and there a house arose on its own green lawn with a proper fence and shrubs. But most of the houses were new, and some of them were just half-finished.

Tracy parked beside one of the newly finished houses and turned her head to smile at Ruth a little apologetically. "I'm afraid I'm showing off," she said. "I couldn't resist showing you my house."

Ruth Ann looked at the house. It wasn't a very big one. It would be about the right size for a woman who lived alone and liked it. She felt cheered all of a sudden. "I love looking at houses," she said. "Do we have time to look around?"

She could see at once that she'd made a mistake. Tracy thought she was trying to be agreeable.

"We'll take time," Tracy said, and slipped from behind the wheel quickly. "Watch out for the loose dirt. There will be a walk through here eventually. The place is supposed to be completed in a little over two weeks." She led the way between the planks that had been set up for the pouring of concrete and let them into the house with a key that she fished from the bottom of her purse.

It was a pleasant house—big windows and a fireplace and rooms that fitted together neatly. There were two good-size bedrooms, but one was situated so that it could double as a study. The kitchen was compact, the closets were huge, and there was a small dining room that opened out onto what could be a patio. There was even an efficient laundry room with loads of storage space.

When they had been planning the dream house for the country estate, one of the things Ruth Ann's mother had insisted on was lots of storage space.

Tracy was having a fine time showing off her house, but finally Ruth Ann's silence got through to her. "I'm probably boring you," she said, and some of the brightness left her face. "We can go now, if you like."

"It's very nice," Ruth Ann said carefully. "So many of the new houses don't have large enough closets or any storage space, but this one is just about perfect." She didn't know what made her say that, except that Tracy had looked so happy just moments before.

"Well anyway, here it is." Tracy was smiling again as she made a sweeping gesture. "Of course, it's hard to picture how it will look with furniture and rugs and drapes."

"It isn't hard at all," Ruth Ann said, half-closing her eyes. "The style should be modern, of course, but not too modern. Very simple drapes, one good pic-

48

ture over the fireplace, and mirrors to reflect the room here and here. And a bright, bright rug . . . red, I think." She opened her eyes, flushed, and bit her lip. "I'm sorry. I was just thinking out loud."

Tracy looked around thoughtfully. "You may be exactly right. Maybe you inherited your mother's ability. Maybe you'll be an interior decorator one day."

"I'm one now," Ruth Ann couldn't resist pointing out. "But unfortunately the only interior I decorate is my own." She patted her stomach by way of illustration, and Tracy chuckled. For the first time her eyes were warm and friendly and not a bit sorry for Ruth Ann.

They went out and got into the car, but Tracy didn't drive off immediately. She sat there, sliding her palms up and down on the wheel, probably trying to think what to say, how to begin.

Ruth Ann wished she had the courage to blurt out all the things that were crowded into her heart. "Why do you want to marry my father?" she could ask. "Why him? You're an attractive woman with a good job and a car and lovely clothes. There must be other men you could marry, so why my father? He was perfectly happy the way he was. He still missed mother, but he was contented. We had a good life. . . ."

But she said nothing of the sort. She just sat there,

dumb, with her hands twisted together in the lap of her blue serge dress.

No one had to tell her that her father was a very attractive man, and it was entirely possible that Tracy was tired of being an old maid, if she *was* an old maid. She could be a widow. The thought was new, and it startled Ruth Ann. "Have you ever been married?"

She was shocked to hear herself blurt out the tactless question, and she tried to soften it by floundering on. "I mean, it seems odd that you haven't married. I always thought that nurses married their patients, and that's why there is always such a shortage of nurses."

Tracy smiled. "Not always, not nearly as often as some people think. As a matter of fact, a great many nurses marry doctors."

"Oh," Ruth Ann said blankly.

Tracy grinned at her, not at all offended by her question. "So now I expect you are wondering why I didn't marry a doctor. But there never seem to be quite enough to go around. And anyway, they were all spoken for by the time I got to be a nurse. That was eight years ago."

Ruth Ann did some rapid mental calculations. Eight years . . . but that meant that Tracy had to be a lot younger than she had supposed.

Tracy was watching her. "I didn't go into nurses' training right after high school," she said, as if she could look inside Ruth Ann's head and see what was going on. "I had a year at the university, and then I took care of my mother until she died. It was a lingering illness, and she could have been quite comfortable in a nursing home. But I didn't want her to go away, and she didn't want to leave. We had only each other. Fortunately, my father had provided for us fairly well. There was enough money set aside for me to finish at the university, but I had already decided that someday I would be a nurse."

"Your father is dead, too?" Ruth Ann asked gently.

"I really couldn't say," Tracy admitted. "He and my mother were divorced when I was quite small. I haven't heard from him in ten or twelve years. I got a Christmas card from Hawaii that time." Something in her tone made Ruth realize that Tracy didn't want to talk about him.

Tracy started the car and turned it toward the freeway. When they were in traffic she spoke again. "Your father told you about our plans," she said, and her words were a statement not a question.

"He said he had asked you to marry him," Ruth Ann replied. "He said you were going to think about it."

Tracy shot a quick glance at the girl's half-averted profile. "And does the idea make you very unhappy, Ruth?"

"It doesn't matter, does it?" she answered.

51

"Whether I approve or not. After all, I've had Father to myself for four years."

"And you'd like to have your life go on like that. It's a perfectly natural way for you to feel. But if you'll stop and think about it, you'll realize that the situation isn't fair to your father or to you."

"Why not?"

"Because everyone needs to be a *person*, Ruth, an independent human being. It's fine to be needed, to feel that you're necessary to the people you love, but it's important to be yourself, too. You can't continue to be a crutch for your father. You don't really want him to be a crutch for you. It's just easier that way." When Ruth Ann didn't answer she went on. "Both of you have been trying to take your mother's place, but you aren't a wife and he isn't a mother. You're kidding yourself if you pretend that it's working out happily."

Ruth Ann flushed. "We have been happy," she said. "We've been very happy . . . until just lately."

Tracy chose to ignore the implication that they had been happy until *she* came along. "I know that you and your father have a wonderful relationship. I knew it even before he brought me home to meet you. But I still contend that a sixteen-year-old girl is not a stimulating companion for a man in his forties, and that it's wrong that you should be cut off from companions in your own age group."

"I don't like kids my own age," Ruth Ann burst out. "I hate teen-agers. They're mean and rude. They laugh at me behind my back and sometimes right to my face. And anyway, I *do* have a companion my own age. Jeanie is my friend."

"But you shouldn't have 'a friend,' you should have a dozen of them. Boys and girls you go to school with, young people in your church group."

"Why?" Ruth Ann asked. "Who needs them?"

"You do." Tracy told her mildly. "Offhand, I can't think of anyone who needs them more."

"I suppose . . . I suppose next thing *you* are going to offer to be my friend," Ruth Ann said ungraciously.

Tracy's fingers tightened on the wheel, but her voice didn't change. "No," she said. "That wasn't what I had in mind. Anyway, friendship isn't a one-way street. It has to be two people coming from opposite directions with their hands outstretched."

There didn't seem to be anything to say after that. They drove the rest of the way in silence. Ruth Ann sat slumped in her corner of the seat feeling more miserable and unattractive with each ticking second. Nothing had been settled, nothing had been resolved.

When they met her father in the lobby of his office building, she felt even worse, because he looked so happy to see them together.

THREE

❦

There were several times during the next weeks when Ruth Ann was almost able to convince herself that she had been worried needlessly. If her father continued to see Tracy, he saw her very briefly, and she never again came to the apartment. Gradually their life settled back into its familiar pattern.

Sometimes Ruth Ann wanted to ask her father what had happened, but she never did. It was enough that he was back again—her friend and her companion, the one person in the world who wasn't critical or overanxious about her. March came in cold and blustering, and April was just around the corner.

Ruth Ann looked forward to the summer when Mrs. Malcome would be going to Canada to visit old friends, and Ruth would be in charge of the apartment. They would go on a lot of picnics, she decided. Her father loved the beach, and even though Ruth Ann didn't swim she could always sit under the beach umbrella and watch him. It was a shame, he said, that Ruth Ann didn't learn to swim. He thought she was afraid of the water, and she never confessed that it wasn't the water she hated so much as seeing herself in a bathing suit.

"I can't wait until summer," she said one evening, when they were settled down before the TV set. "Do you suppose we'll have any good weekends before school is out?"

"It's hard to say," her father murmured, only half listening.

"Not that I'm so crazy about the hot weather," Ruth Ann went on. "But you always look so rested after a day at the beach. You've been looking tired lately."

He looked at her thoughtfully. "I'm getting older. That might account for it."

"Oh pooh, you aren't old at all. Forty is supposed to be the . . . the prime of a man's life, isn't it?"

"Is it?" he countered without smiling.

She felt a sharp thrust of alarm. Maybe it was the shadow of the lamps, but for the moment her father looked almost old. Not just unhappy, but tired and bored as well. The thought jolted her, because if he was bored. . . . "Dad, are you sure you feel all right," she asked quietly. "That ulcer hasn't been bothering you again. . . ."

He waved the ulcer away with a flick of his fingers and settled back to watch television once more, but

Ruth found it hard to concentrate on the figures on the screen. Her eyes were drawn again and again to her father's face. It seemed to her that it was thinner, and unless it was a trick of the lighting there was a sprinkle more gray in his hair.

He doesn't look a bit happy, she told herself at last. I haven't let myself see it, because I haven't wanted to see it. I wonder how long it's been since he really laughed about something . . . about anything?

When the program was over and while her father was still glancing at the TV, she made herself ask the question. "Tracy Emery hasn't been around for a while. Is she on a new case?"

He looked up warily. "Not that I know of. I had lunch with her a couple of days ago."

It was perfectly clear that he wasn't going to say any more about it. But at least Ruth had established that he was still seeing Tracy, that he was still interested. Before she went to bed she came back to the subject doggedly. "You said that you'd asked Tracy to marry you and that she'd promised to think about it. Does this mean that she's still trying to make up her mind?"

"I hope so," he said gravely. "But I imagine what she's doing is giving *you* some time to think about it." He didn't speak reproachfully, but Ruth Ann felt her cheeks burn.

"I don't know why she should worry about that. I have nothing to say in the matter."

"Tracy thinks you do," he said.

If he had said, "I think you do" or even "we think you do" it wouldn't have been so bad, but he was making it obvious that the decision was Tracy's.

"Anyway," Ruth said recklessly, to cover the feeling of loss and hurt, "anyway, she doesn't have to concern herself about me. I'll be eighteen in a couple of years. She ought to be able to stand me underfoot for two years."

Her father didn't answer at once, but he reached over and clicked off the television. When at last he turned in his chair to look at her, his eyes were the eyes of a stranger, cold and measuring.

Ruth Ann stood first on one foot and then the other, the way she did when she was nervous. She probably looked like an overweight, ill-at-ease stork, she told herself bitterly. She really couldn't blame her father if he was comparing her to Tracy, who would never in the world be guilty of such a peevish statement.

"You resent Tracy," he said. "You've made it perfectly clear that you resent her, but you are at least smart enough to realize that this isn't a question of being able to stand one another underfoot. When I marry Tracy, it will be a real marriage and we will be a real family."

57

"You mean you wouldn't marry her if I didn't agree?" she demanded incredulously.

He shook his head. "I didn't say that. I said that Tracy wouldn't marry me."

Ruth Ann gulped and swallowed and the words she wanted to say wouldn't come out. Finally she turned and went to her room, moving blindly so that she bumped her thigh against a table that had been standing right there for ages. She was so hurt and confused that she was scarcely aware of hitting the table.

The night was long and her sleep was broken into nightmarish fragments. It was very late when she heard her father go out. She padded barefoot through the darkened apartment and watched until his car pulled out of the apartment garage, roared off down the street, and disappeared around the corner.

She went back to bed feeling shaken. So that was why she hadn't known he was still seeing Tracy. She was probably working a day shift, and he saw her late in the evening, after Ruth Ann was asleep. This schedule might have been going on for weeks. Where did they meet? What did they talk about? Tracy's house was probably finished by now. Did she invite him over for cozy late suppers before the new fireplace?

What they did wasn't any of her business, of

course, she'd be the first to admit that, but just the same he might have at least mentioned seeing Tracy. He might have said, "Tracy's moving into her house this weekend. Why don't we go out there and help shove the furniture around?" If he *wanted* his daughter to feel shut out and unwanted, this was certainly the right way to go about it!

But even as she felt the tight lump of tears in her throat, Ruth Ann knew that she was being unfair. She hadn't ever indicated that she wanted to be a part of the life he shared with Tracy. She had avoided the subject in the mistaken notion that if she didn't let herself believe that Tracy was important, the hope would become a fact.

She was still awake much later when she heard her father let himself into the apartment and go straight to his room. Sometimes when he worked late he raided the refrigerator before he went to bed. And a few times, when the light was still on in Ruth's room and he knew she was reading, he'd knock on her door softly, and then look in to say good-night. Once in a while he invited her to slip on her robe and come out and keep him company while he ate. Ruth Ann's heart ached thinking about those old happy times.

The next morning Ruth's father left for work before her alarm went off. He didn't even call good-by.

She thought about staying home from school and pleading illness, but it was Mrs. Malcome's cleaning day; she'd be coming in around ten o'clock and fussing at Ruth all the time she was there. It was easier to get dressed and go to school as usual.

She waited until she was sure Jeanie had gone on, though. She wasn't in the mood for Jeanie's sprightly conversation—or even her sympathetic gloom.

Ruth Ann had to walk faster than usual in order to reach school before the tardy bell, and she was out of breath and panting when she arrived. Usually she and Jeanie arranged to be there early so that they avoided the heaviest flow of traffic in the congested halls. This morning she seemed to be blocking the way every time she turned a corridor; boys and girls made large detours around her. Some of them grinned back over their shoulder and a few made pointed remarks that Ruth Ann chose to ignore. She plodded along toward her homeroom, her books clutched firmly in one arm.

A small girl in a bright sweater and matching skirt whirled past her, and almost at once a boy followed. "Hey, wait up, pip-squeak," he called, and the girl scowled at him, but waited until he reached her side before they moved on. They walked along more slowly then, their heads almost touching and their muted voices and laughter drifting back to Ruth Ann following awkwardly at their heels.

How wonderful to have someone call to you like

that! "Hey, wait up, pip-squeak." Ruth Ann sighed and turned into her room, finding her seat just seconds before the tardy bell sounded.

She was always on time and she always had her homework assignments, but she would never be a really outstanding student. Her father said it was because she was too shy to assert herself, but she knew it wasn't anything like that. She just wasn't that interested in school, and thus far she had no idea what she wanted to do with her life when school was behind her. There would be at least a year at the university, her father insisted on that, and there would probably be enough to see her through if she wanted to continue her studies and become a teacher. When she was younger, while her mother was living, they had talked about Ruth Ann's being a teacher, but that had been when she was a chubby ten- and twelve-year-old. It wasn't until the last three or four years that Ruth had become so alarmingly big.

"Well, where were *you* this morning?" Jeanie greeted her, when they met in the lunchroom at the usual time. "I waited until twenty minutes to, and then I had to fly. What happened?"

"I guess I was mooning around and didn't realize what time it was," Ruth said not quite truthfully. "I didn't sleep very well. Dad and I had kind of an argument."

She waited for Jeanie to ask what the argument

61

had been about, but the other girl's attention was diverted by the display of desserts in the cafeteria lineup. "Oh boy, look at that peach cobbler," she murmured. "I'm going to have some of that. Do you suppose it's real whipped cream or that low calorie junk?"

Ruth Ann pushed her tray glumly along the track. "I don't think I'll have dessert," she said. "I'm trying another diet."

Jeanie looked martyred. "You know perfectly well you won't stick to a diet," she pointed out. "How about a ham sandwich?"

"I'll have soup," Ruth Ann said firmly. "And a salad, a green salad."

They carried their trays back to the table where they usually ate, but even before the trays were unloaded Ruth was sorry she hadn't followed Jeanie's example and taken the creamed chicken on biscuit. She finished her soup and her salad, but she still felt hungry. Jeanie reported, with some satisfaction, that the whip cream on the peach cobbler was real.

The trouble with diets, Ruth reflected as she went back to her afternoon classes, was that it took so long to get results. If she lost ten pounds, the difference would scarcely show, and it would take weeks and weeks to lose twenty pounds. Losing twenty pounds, though, would bring her down to—well, within striking distance of a hundred and fifty. One forty would be better, and one thirty would be ideal. A girl five foot six who had one hundred and thirty pounds distributed in the right places would be almost thin. At least, she could wear decent-looking clothes and she'd be able to find a bathing suit that *fit!* She was so engrossed in her thoughts that Mr. Graham had to ask twice if she would translate the first two paragraphs of the Latin assignment, and then when she was on her feet she became so flustered that she made half a dozen mistakes in the lesson she had known perfectly at home.

She hurried back to the apartment as soon as school was dismissed, not even waiting for Jeanie, who would stop for an ice-cream cone.

Mrs. Malcome had left, but the apartment gave shining evidence of her earlier visit. The walls and tile in the bathroom were shining, and the sharp clean smell of soap powder and ammonia lingered in all the rooms. The kitchen floor was freshly scrubbed and waxed. Ruth Ann told herself that the wax wasn't completely dry. That way she wouldn't be tempted to look in the refrigerator.

She went around the apartment and opened the windows, not even looking at the fruit in the bowl on the dining-room table. Everyone knew that fruit filled a person with water and made him heavier than ever. Jeanie was always telling her that. Why Jeanie had an aunt who lost thirty pounds in six weeks, and *she* said. . . .

The telephone rang and she answered it. The call

was from her father saying that he was staying in town for dinner. "You'll be all right, won't you?" He asked the usual question. "You'll remember to lock both doors and not open them until you're sure who's there?"

"Yes, I'll remember," she said listlessly. "Will you be very late?"

"I don't know." He sounded rushed. "Fix yourself something luscious for dinner. O.K.?"

"O.K.," she said.

She hung up the phone and went out into the kitchen to look in the refrigerator. There were always frozen chops and steaks on hand, and there was practically an entire pie that Mrs. Malcome had made the day before. Ruth Ann was the only one who had eaten any of it, but the missing wedge looked pretty big, almost a quarter of the pie.

Resolutely she shut the refrigerator door. She was aware that her stomach was sending out distress signals, but suffering gave her a curious sense of accomplishment. If she did lose a lot of weight, her father and Tracy would realize how unfair they were leaving the important decision of their life in her hands.

Fix yourself something luscious for dinner, her father had said. As if having something luscious to eat could make up for everything.

Let's stop and have a luscious sundae, he used to

say when they were coming home from a sad movie. How about a deluxe hamburger, he had tempted her the evening she was feeling so downhearted because she wasn't invited to a party one of the girls at school was giving.

Ruth Ann sank back in her chair and stared at the ceiling glumly. She knew all about the psychology of overeating. People ate too much because they were bored, or because they were unhappy, or because they needed to make up for some lack in their life. All the reasons sounded perfectly logical on paper, but she had never stopped to think about them as they applied to her. She sat up a little straighter. It was really her father's fault that she was so fat, when you came right down to it. Her father was always offering her food as a substitute for the things he couldn't give her—the companionship of a mother, popularity in her own age group. He brought her boxes of candy instead of pretty sweaters; he took her to fine restaurants to make up for her lack of dates. Not that it was entirely fair to blame the whole thing on her father; he was just trying to make her feel loved and wanted.

The ring of the doorbell cut through her troubled thoughts, and for a moment she considered not answering. Whoever it was would get tired after a while and go away. But when the ring was repeated, her curiosity wouldn't let her remain sitting there in the peaceful half dark. She got to her feet and went to open the door.

Tracy was standing there, and she looked disapproving as well as worried. "Ruth, I'm sure your father has told you about *not* opening the door when you aren't sure who's ringing the bell."

"I forgot," Ruth Ann said. "I guess I was thinking about something else." She stepped aside and Tracy came into the apartment. "I thought you were having dinner with my father," she went on bluntly. "When he called and said he wouldn't be able to make it for dinner, I thought that was why."

Tracy smiled. "No. He had a business appointment. I knew you'd be alone, so I thought it might be a good time for you and me to have a little talk." She glanced past Ruth into the kitchen. "Have you had your dinner?"

"I've had all I want," Ruth Ann said.

She watched Tracy settle herself comfortably on the davenport, and she couldn't help feeling a tug of annoyance that Tracy should fit so easily into the apartment. It was still, in Ruth Ann's eyes, her mother's home.

"I had lunch with your father today," Tracy said into a growing silence. "We talked about you."

Ruth Ann waited, not sure of herself or of what she was expected to answer. Tracy Emery didn't seem to feel that an answer was necessary. She went on as casually as if she were thinking aloud. "I've had a splendid offer from a hospital in New Orleans. A couple of years ago I'd have jumped at the chance."

"But now you don't want to go," Ruth Ann supplied, when Tracy stopped and looked at her.

"That's right. Now I'm not sure that I want to go."

"Because of Father?"

"Because of many things, but that most of all," Tracy admitted, and waited.

When the silence had stretched out for an interminably long time, Ruth Ann spoke. "Father seems to think that you're waiting for my blessing or some stupid thing like that."

Tracy looked at her unsmilingly. "Do you really think it's so stupid?"

"In a way I do," Ruth Ann answered with complete honesty. "Because I could keep you from marrying my father for years and years."

"No, not for years and years, but forever," Tracy corrected her gently. "I'm not that young, Ruth, and neither is your father. That's why I thought we should have this talk, because if you are finally and unalterably opposed to this marriage, I will take the position in New Orleans."

Ruth Ann's first feeling of relief was blotted out by uncertainty. "But . . . you'd come back. I mean, you'd come back eventually."

Tracy shook her head. "No. I don't plan to come

67

back. I have no ties here, no roots. Perhaps I'll find some in New Orleans, but I certainly won't find them if I keep looking back over my shoulder. No, if I go away it will be a clean break."

Ruth Ann chewed her underlip nervously. "Father would hate me if he thought it was my fault you went away."

Tracy looked unimpressed. "I suppose so. He'd hate me for a while, too, but he'd get over it. He knows as well as I do that none of us would be happy under these circumstances." She got to her feet then, as if everything had been said, and she looked at Ruth Ann gravely as she gathered up her handbag and gloves. "I'm sorry if I seem to be leaving too much of this in your hands, Ruth, but I'm more sensitive to the role you play in this marriage than you would believe." She did smile then, but it was a mere twisting of her lips; her eyes were still somber. "I'll tell you about it someday, if you want to hear the story."

Ruth Ann got up, feeling awkward and uncomfortable. When Tracy moved toward the door, she followed and spoke woodenly. "Thank you for coming to see me," she said. "Am I supposed to tell Father you were here?"

Tracy looked surprised. "That's entirely up to you, Ruth. You may tell him or not, just as you choose."

When she had gone, Ruth was even more mixed up and unhappy than she had been earlier, and she was so hungry that she was getting a bad headache. She clicked on the TV set and, while waiting for it to warm up, went out to the kitchen and cut herself a big wedge of Mrs. Malcome's apple pie.

It wasn't fair, she told herself. Tracy Emery had no right to put her in the position of judge and jury. Tracy shouldn't expect her to say that she was happy about having her father bring a strange woman into their life, into their home. Did they want her to lie about it?

But how could she bear to be the one responsible for her father's unhappiness if Tracy went away? Suppose he never forgave her? Wouldn't Tracy be as much between them? Maybe she would be even more of an alien presence than she was now.

Ruth Ann sat down and watched television and had another piece of pie and after that an orange and a big glass of milk. Later she couldn't even remember what program she had seen.

When her father came in she didn't get out of her chair. Then, as he came over to brush his hand across her head, in the familiar gesture that had carried over from her pig-tailed days, she couldn't bear it a moment longer.

She started to cry, great noisy sobs that tore at her throat and filled her chest with an aching weight.

Ruth hadn't cried for a long, long time—not really cried—and she could see that her father was terribly upset. He knelt down before her chair, dabbed at her tears with his handkerchief, and made ineffectual soothing sounds. After a long time she managed to stop crying, but she was still sobbing when he went out into the kitchen and brought her a drink of water.

"There, that's better," he said, but his eyes were still concerned. "Now, do you want to talk about it or will it wait until another time?"

Her father looked sweet and worried, and his voice was gentle. She looked at him with new eyes and wondered why she had tried to tell herself that he was happy. There were lines in his face that hadn't been there a year ago, and his eyes were tired, as if all the sleep in the world couldn't really rest him.

"I'm sorry," she gulped. "I haven't been thinking of you or Tracy or . . . or anyone but me. I'm jealous. That's what's the matter. I can't bear to think of your loving someone more than you love me."

He smiled and touched her wet cheek affectionately, pushing back the lock of hair that had fallen forward. "Ruth Ann, no one can ever take your place, you know that. In a few years you'll meet a boy, a man by that time, and you'll fall in love and get married. Does that mean you'll stop loving me?"

"Of course not," she said.

He nodded. "Well then . . ." he said, as if everything was settled. He didn't seem to think it funny that he had suggested some boy, some man, would fall in love with her and want to marry her. He made it sound perfectly reasonable.

Much later, after they had talked for a long, long time about the changes that would be necessary in their life, he went to the phone and called Tracy. "This is a formal invitation," Ruth Ann heard him say. "My daughter and I would like to have you come for dinner tomorrow evening. Can you come?" She couldn't hear Tracy's reply, but it seemed to please her father. He laughed, and it was his old, joyous laugh.

She held down the swift stab of jealousy. I have to meet her halfway, she reminded herself. We can't be friends if I resent every word my father speaks to her, every laugh they share.

If I loved Tracy I wouldn't have any problem. But I don't love her; I don't even *like* her, and maybe I never will. So I'll have to work extra hard at being her friend. If she's willing to come toward me with both hands outstretched, I should be able to do the same thing. For Father, because we both love him and he loves both of us.

FOUR

In the hectic days that followed it seemed impossible that so many things could be accomplished in such a short time.

"This is the jet age," Ruth Ann's father reminded her and Tracy, when they tried to point out that these things took *time*. "You get a license, buy some rings, find someone to marry you, and invite a few friends to attend the ceremony. That's all there is to it."

The wedding was to be very simple. It would take place in the church, of course, but with only a handful of close friends in attendance and with Ruth Ann as the maid of honor.

She hadn't wanted to be the maid of honor. She had honestly tried to get out of it, but on this one point her father was unexpectedly firm. "If you refuse, Tracy can think only one thing: that you are unhappy about this marriage, that you still resent having her come into our life."

"But that isn't true," Ruth Ann protested. "I want

72

you to be happy, and you're happy when you're with Tracy. I haven't seen you so happy since . . . since. . . ." She broke off, but he finished the thought quietly.

"Since your mother died."

"Yes," Ruth Ann whispered.

He patted her shoulder, and then went to stare out the window, the way he always did when he was deeply moved. When he spoke again his voice was thoughtful, "I was very happy with your mother, Ruth Ann. When she died a part of my life, a very good part of my life, was over. But I had you, and you were a reason for going on and making life as sweet as possible for the two of us." He turned his head to smile at her, and she nodded to show she understood what he was trying to say. "I never expected to find anyone else. Even now it's a little hard for me to believe. But we'll have a good life together, you and Tracy and me."

After that, she couldn't refuse to be maid of honor.

She was glad the wedding was going to be in April. April seemed like a good month for a new beginning.

Tracy took her along when she picked out her wedding suit, an oyster white suit with pale blue gloves and a hat with a wisp of veiling. "I hope you don't think I'm silly wanting a white suit," she told Ruth Ann, as they waited for the saleswoman to

73

bring in some of the newer models. "I expect old dreams die hard, and as a young girl I always dreamed of being married in white satin and lace."

When it came time to buy the suit Ruth would wear, Tracy knew exactly what she wanted. "Nonsense, of course you won't wear navy blue. You can wear all the navy blue you want when you are older. Yellow would be lovely with your skin and hair. Let's look at yellow."

Ruth Ann's protests dwindled as they looked at the yellow suits. There was one—not really a suit but a sheath type dress with a coat length sleeveless jacket —that she liked very much. The price tag was staggering, but Tracy waved away her protests.

"Your father said we could go all out, and we're going all out," she declared gaily. She made Ruth turn around and around for her inspection and nodded as if well pleased by what she saw. "Yes, it's very nice, and when you lose some more weight, it will be easy enough to take it in."

And in the meantime, Ruth Ann told herself pivoting slowly befor the full-length mirror, she would look like a pale yellow blimp. She had to admit, though, that the color was good on her and that the long coat was much better than a regular suit.

The days slipped by smoothly, but each one held surprises. The week before the wedding Tracy was

74

at the Callahans' apartment every day when Ruth came in from school. She didn't have to be there, but still it was nice to have her. She showed Ruth all the wedding gifts—from the people who had known Tracy at the hospital and the people Ruth Ann's father worked with—as they arrived. Sometimes Tracy didn't even know the person who had sent the gift. The beautiful mother-of-pearl table centerpiece from Mr. and Mrs. Conners was one such surprise. Ruth Ann explained that Mr. Conners was her father's lawyer, but that they were old friends, too. They used to golf together.

In spite of herself she felt close to Tracy during these days. If it was true that trouble drew people close together, it was probably just as true that happiness shared had the same effect.

"I told you it wouldn't be so bad if you'd try to look on the bright side," Jeanie reminded her smugly, when Ruth Ann tried to explain something of this feeling. "After all, it isn't as if your stepmother will be sitting around keeping her eagle eye on you. She'll go on working, won't she?"

"I don't know," Ruth Ann said. "We haven't discussed it."

"Well maybe *you* haven't, but you can bet that they have," Jeanie said. "After all, it would be pretty strange if they discussed everything with you."

"It wouldn't be strange at all. We're going to be a real family." Ruth Ann spoke as if she really believed what she was saying, as if she never had twinges of doubt, as if she never suffered a single pang of jealousy.

She was going to stay on at the apartment with Mrs. Malcome while Tracy and her father drove to Palm Springs for a honeymoon. They would only be gone for one week, because that was all the time her father could afford to take in the spring of the year, but later on, in the summer, they would take another short trip. The three of them.

Tracy's clothes and her favorite pieces of furniture were moved into the apartment. The other furniture and household things were to be sent to one of her pet charities. She said someone might as well use them.

There was a beautiful desk with a matching chair, and a heavy hand-carved chest of some reddish wood, which stood on curled claw feet. A friend had brought it from China and given it to Tracy while she was still a girl in school. "Mother always called it my hope chest," she told Ruth Ann, as the girl leaned down to admire the fanciful carving. "In my mother's day all proper young ladies had hope chests."

"They did?" Ruth Ann said vaguely. "Why?"

Tracy shrugged. "I expect it was carried over from

76

the old country custom of a bride having a dowry. The general idea was that the chest should be filled with fine tablecloths and napkins and embroidered pieces. Mostly things that the girls made themselves, things that were really too nice to be used for everyday, so they saved them for their future homes."

"Why?" Ruth Ann asked again, and Tracy grinned.

"I expect a lot of girls wondered why. Anyway, hope chests, as such, aren't in favor nowadays."

Tracy's house would be either rented or sold as soon as the lawn grew in and the landscaping was completed. Tracy seemed entirely indifferent to the thought that another woman would be living in the house she had helped to plan.

Tracy's lovely clothes filled two thirds of the master bedroom closet. She was a little apologetic about the space they took when she was putting them away with Ruth Ann a fascinated spectator. "It must seem to you that I have far too many clothes," she said. "But there was such a long time when I couldn't have these pretty things that I guess I went overboard."

Ruth Ann waited, but she didn't explain why she hadn't been able to have nice things for a long time. Ruth Ann filed away her question mentally as something she must remember to ask her father.

She still wasn't quite comfortable with Tracy.

77

First and foremost there was the question of what to call her. Tracy was too informal to be called Mother, and she certainly didn't want to say that anyway. Ruth Ann found that she was detouring around using any name at all, but the issue had to be faced sooner or later. When she talked to other people she could refer to Tracy as "my stepmother" or "my father's wife," but she couldn't carry these terms over into their family life.

The wedding service would be performed in a small church where Tracy had once attended Sunday School. Ruth Ann was glad that there would be only a few people to watch her walk down the aisle. One of the doctors at the hospital had volunteered to give the bride away, but Tracy said she preferred to give herself away. And then she smiled at Ruth Ann's father and added, "Gladly."

No one noticed that Ruth Ann managed to lose eight pounds. It wasn't surprising, because she could hardly notice it herself. Whenever she got especially hungry she went into her bedroom and looked at the yellow suit in its plastic bag. Since that first Monday when she had skipped having a milk shake with Jeanie, she had made one excuse after another to avoid afternoon snacks. And she had foresworn candy bars, because she was saving her money for something special. She could have asked her father, of course, he'd have been delighted to let her have an advance on her allowance, especially if she explained that she wanted to buy a gift for Tracy, but that would spoil it. The gesture had to be entirely her own doing. A hand outstretched in friendship, a tacit apology, because it wasn't truly a gift of love.

On Saturday she didn't have luncheon in town and go to a first-run movie with Jeanie. She told Jeanie that she had some things to attend to, and she could see that Jeanie was furious.

Ruth Ann took a long walk in the park that afternoon. She watched the animals and inspected the flower gardens and kept out of the way of the little sight-seeing cars that zipped back and forth. She had purposely left her money at home so she wouldn't be tempted to buy an ice-cream cone or a hamburger, but she could have cried when she saw other people eating. Finally she returned home and found that her father and Tracy were still out. They had gone shopping for her father's new suit. She went out into the kitchen and made herself three peanut-butter-and-jelly sandwiches. She could have eaten three more, but she was already hating herself. As punishment she wouldn't eat any dessert that night, and she could see that the refusal worried her father.

"Sure you feel O.K., honey?" he asked. "When you turn down chocolate cake, it has to be something desperate. . . ."

"I just don't *want* any," she snapped, because she

79

did want some of that cake and no one but an idiot would question her reasons. She weighed a hundred and seventy pounds, probably more after all that peanut butter and jelly, and she was going to wear an expensive beautiful yellow suit and look like the Goodyear blimp at the wedding. Men were so . . . so . . . stupid.

School went on as usual. No one told her that she looked thinner. No one stopped to ask her about the coming wedding or how she felt about having a stepmother. For the past couple of years she had turned aside any offer of friendship. She had been afraid of being laughed at, and even more afraid of having people be nice to her because they were sorry for her. So now, when she would have welcomed the interest of her classmates, no one even bothered.

There was Jeanie, of course, but a little coldness had grown up between them. It had started when Jeanie invited her over to work on some class assignments, and Ruth Ann hadn't wanted to go.

"Why don't you want to come?" Jeanie had demanded, and Ruth Ann responded with perfect truth.

"Because I'm trying to give up sweets, and you will tempt me beyond my strength, that's why. You know perfectly well that you have cookies and candy bars stashed away all over the house."

"No one is going to twist your arm," Jeanie assured her. "If you want to go on another idiotic diet that won't do you a particle of good, I'm sure it doesn't make a speck of difference to me!"

"Oh, have a heart, Jeanie. You know how hard it is for me to resist food. I'm just trying to keep out of temptation, that's all. I have *finally* made up my mind that I'm not going to be a comic cartoon any longer, and the least you can do is give me moral support."

Jeanie seemed to swell with anger. *"Well,"* she said, "if you don't care for my company you can just say so. You don't have to be insulting about it."

"I wasn't being. . . ."

"You were too. You practically called me a comic cartoon to my face!"

The quarrel blew over in a few days.

Ruth Ann caught up with Jeanie walking home from school one afternoon and tried to start a normal conversation. Common sense told her that the best thing to do was to ignore the earlier unpleasantness. It didn't help matters that Jeanie made a big production of trying to hide the candy bar she was eating. "Oh, pardon *me,*" she said. "I really didn't mean to tempt you beyond your strength."

"Don't be silly," Ruth Ann said. "I wanted to explain about that. You know how much we spend on sundaes and candy bars and things like that. Well, I just can't afford it, because I've been saving my money for something special."

"For a size-ten dress?" Jeanie asked sweetly.

Ruth Ann shook her head. It was hard not to get mad at Jeanie when she was being so childish. "No, a bridal gift for Tracy."

"You mean a wedding gift."

Ruth Ann shook her head again. "No, a bridal gift. You know how it is when girls get married. Their friends get together and give them bridal showers. The bride gets things for her house and sometimes fancy personal items that look . . . well, bridelike."

"You mean you're giving a shower for your *stepmother?*"

"Of course not. And anyway, she isn't my stepmother yet."

She was sorry she'd said anything about it. Jeanie was determined to cling to her injured feelings, so let her cling.

But Jeanie was watching her with curiosity mixed with awe. "Honestly, Ruth Ann, sometimes I wonder about you. You were so sure you didn't want a stepmother, and then you went ahead and gave them your blessing when you could have *stopped* the wedding. Now you want to give her a bridal shower."

"I told you I wasn't. I just want to give her a nice gift. Something she's wanted for a long time."

"Now what could you possibly give her that she

couldn't buy for herself?" Jeanie demanded reasonably.

That was the trouble with trying to talk to Jeanie. No matter how good and uplifted you felt, Jeanie could cut you down with a word or a grin or even a lifted eyebrow.

That very evening Ruth Ann went downtown after school and visited an exclusive shop for Tracy's gift. She explained to the haughty saleswoman that she had seen it in the window a few weeks before. She needed it in a size twelve, and if she didn't have quite enough to pay for it she'd make a deposit and pick it up later. The twenty-five dollars with her, she realized, might not be enough.

It wasn't enough. What she had seen was made of imported Italian lace and cost almost fifty dollars. When she explained who the gift was for, the woman melted somewhat and found her a similar item that was less than the money she had saved. Of course, the lace wasn't imported. . . .

When she took the package home, Tracy was in the bedroom putting some of her things in a chest of drawers. She looked surprised when Ruth handed her the gift-wrapped box, but at least she didn't say, "For *me?* Oh, Ruth you really shouldn't. . . ." She just thanked the girl gravely and read the card.

Ruth Ann had labored over what to say on the card, but she hoped it sounded spontaneous.

"For Tracy, on her wedding day. If you want to

wear lace and white satin, I don't see why you shouldn't. I hope you will be very happy." She had hesitated a long time before she had signed it simply "Ruth." It seemed a little hypocritical to add the word *love*.

Tracy opened the box and saw the lovely satin slip and panties. The lace was almost as fine as the imported lace. Maybe someday she would tell Tracy about the other set, the one she had seen in the window. Tracy took out the slip and smoothed it between her hands. She looked as if she wanted to cry.

"It's the right size," Ruth Ann said in a very small voice. "I checked to be sure."

"It's beautiful." Tracy said. "It's lovely, Ruth Ann. I will wear it for something new. Thank you."

She was glad that Tracy didn't feel she had to say more. Gushing over the gift would have embarrassed both of them.

When she told Jeanie what she had given Tracy, Jeanie thought she was out of her mind. "If you gave her a locket or a bracelet it would be something she could *show* to people. But she can't go around showing people her slip and pants!"

Ruth sighed. "It doesn't matter if she shows anyone, silly. The important thing is that she wanted to be married in lace and white satin, and now she will be. That's what's important."

Jeanie shook her head. "It still sounds like a funny wedding present to me."

"A bridal gift," Ruth corrected her gently. "The wedding gift was even more special. I gave her my father."

It was the day before the wedding, and then it was the wedding day.

When Ruth Ann was getting into the yellow suit, she was sorry that Tracy wasn't there to see how easily it zipped. At least, the zipper noticed the eight missing pounds.

A friend of Tracy's was picking her up, and she was meeting Ruth Ann and her father at the church. Mrs. Malcome was all excited and wanted them to eat a hearty breakfast, even though there was to be a wedding breakfast at a hotel after the ceremony. Mrs. Malcome talked and talked and talked, but Ruth Ann said very little. When they were going out to get into the car, her father gave her a bouquet of yellow roses, and then he leaned over and kissed her. No one had to explain that he was saying good-by to all the happy times they had shared. She wished that she could tell him the happy times would be even happier when Tracy was with them. She wished she could really believe so.

The ceremony was over in a matter of minutes. Afterward Ruth could hardly remember anything about it. All she carried away with her was the smile her father was wearing when he kissed Tracy and then turned to kiss her.

After the wedding breakfast her father drove her and Mrs. Malcome back to the apartment. Ruth Ann got out of the car, still holding the bouquet of roses, and managed a good-by smile that was good enough to fool all of them.

"You behave yourself," her father admonished her cheerfully. "You have the address if you have to reach us in an emergency, and we'll call in a couple of days to check up on you."

Tracy sat in her corner of the front seat, holding her wedding bouquet as if it were made of glass.

"Good-by," Ruth Ann said. "Have a good time." And then she stopped and chewed her lip, because that didn't sound quite right.

Tracy smiled. "Good-by, Ruth. And thank you again . . . for everything. I love my gift."

"What gift?" Ruth Ann's father demanded immediately. "This is the first I've heard of it. No one gave me a wedding gift."

"I'll bake you a wedding cake," Ruth Ann promised. "I'll make your favorite cake and bake it in tiers, and when you get back we can get out that special bottle of br—" She stopped then, wishing the earth would open and swallow her. How could she have said such a thing? What was the matter with her? She hadn't even been *thinking* about that bottle of brandy.

But her father's eyes scarcely flickered. "That's right," he said. "I'd almost forgotten the brandy."

When the car had driven away, Ruth followed Mrs. Malcome up to the apartment, which already seemed chill and lonely. "I feel," she said, as Mrs. Malcome puttered around, adjusting the blinds and rearranging things on the coffee table, "I feel as if I might be coming unglued."

Mrs. Malcome gave her a quick smile. "Perfectly natural reaction, my girl. You've been living on excitement these past weeks, and now you're let down. What you need is a hearty lunch and a nice nap." Then she straightened up and looked at Ruth Ann curiously. "What was all that about a bottle of brandy?"

Ruth Ann sat down on the arm of the davenport dejectedly. "I could cut my own throat. I just didn't stop to *think*. When Mother and Dad came back from that trip to Mexico years and years ago, they brought a beautiful decanter bottle of special brandy. They said they were going to save it for a very important occasion. Only the occasions never seemed quite special enough. Mother always said, 'Oh no, let's save it.' And then, after she died, Father took it out of the sideboard and hid it away somewhere. I don't know what made me mention it. It must have been subconscious or something."

Mrs. Malcome clucked sympathetically. "Well, it's the sort of thing anyone might blurt out without thinking. I'm sure your father didn't mind."

"But *I* mind," Ruth Ann said. "I'm just awkward, that's all. I fall over my own feet and talk without even knowing what I'm going to say. I'm just a *mess*."

"My goodness, aren't we sorry for ourselves," Mrs. Malcome said with scant sympathy, and went to take off her hat and coat and hang them away in the room she was to occupy during her stay. It wasn't exactly a guest room or a study, but it had a comfortable fold-out bed, and Mrs. Malcome said she'd be as comfortable as a bug in a rug. She was always saying things like that. For a while these little whimseys of Mrs. Malcome's had fascinated Ruth Ann, but now she was tired of them. Sometimes she felt that if she had to hear Mrs. Malcome's expressions *one more time,* she would simply explode.

She expected the week would be long and dull, and it was. Mrs. Malcome was nice enough, but she told the same stories over and over and over. Stories about people Ruth Ann had never even met. Her distant cousins, her old school chums, and the "girls" who had shared her young-married days, as well as all the anecdotes about the late Mr. Malcome, may he rest in peace.

Jeanie didn't come to visit. She made no secret of the fact that she couldn't stand Mrs. Malcome, and Ruth Ann was too polite—or maybe too stupid—to leave Mrs. Malcome by herself while she went off to visit Jeanie. They spent long evenings watching television, because Mrs. Malcome was an avid TV fan, and stereo music made her nervous.

It should have been an excellent time for Ruth to stick to her self-imposed diet. She even planned how surprised and pleased her father would be when he returned and found her looking so much better. Only things didn't work out that way. She found herself eating when she wasn't even *hungry,* and Mrs. Malcome didn't say a word. Clearly she had given up on Ruth Ann months ago.

The third day there was a letter from Tracy, and almost every day after that a postcard or a small gift. A lacy handkerchief slipped into an envelope with a note from her father—"This is for show and not for blow." Ruth Ann smiled when she read it. Poor Father, he was almost as corny as Mrs. Malcome. Tracy sent her a small ivory figure, a lucky piece, and a soft Angora head scarf that framed her face becomingly. When Ruth Ann draped it just right she looked almost pretty—hardly fat at all—but when she took off the scarf and her own wide face looked back at her, she could have wept with disappointment.

They were coming back on Friday, and she was really looking forward to the day.

"Sometime after noon," her father assured her when he called on Wednesday evening. "How have you been getting along, Ruthy?"

"I'm just fine," she told him. "Lonesome, though. I'm glad you're coming home."

"We miss you, too," he told her, and she knew that Tracy was probably standing right beside him and that she was expected to say something about *her*.

"I got all the cards and letters," Ruth Ann said. "Tell Tracy I loved the Chinese figure and the head scarf."

"She's right here," her father said heartily. "I'll let you tell her yourself."

Ruth Ann tightened her hold on the receiver when Tracy's soft, "Hello, Ruth," came across the line.

"Hello," Ruth said. "I'm glad you're coming home, and I want to thank you for the cards and gifts." Her voice sounded stiff and she knew it, but in spite of all her brave resolutions about meeting Tracy halfway she hated to think of Tracy with her father, sharing his moods and joining in his laughter.

She was very quiet after they had said good-night and hung up. So quiet that even Mrs. Malcome noticed it. "Did your stepmother say something to upset you?" she asked tactlessly.

"Of course not," Ruth Ann said. "What could she say to upset me, for goodness sakes?"

90

She went into the kitchen and made herself a ham sandwich and poured a large glass of milk to go with it—just to show Mrs. Malcome that she wasn't the least bit upset.

She got through Thursday and even went to bed early, missing one of Mrs. Malcome's favorite shows, so that Friday would come sooner.

On Friday she was almost late to school, because at the last moment she remembered that they might be home before she got back, and she wanted to have fresh flowers in the apartment. Mrs. Malcome said that she could attend to them, but Ruth Ann wanted to get them herself. There was a little flower shop only a block from the apartment. The owner was sweeping up and tending to the plants when Ruth hurried in.

She selected fresh flowers for the glass bowl on the sideboard and a nosegay of violets to put on the dressing table in the bedroom. She didn't have much time to work on the arrangement, but she knew her father would appreciate the gesture. It was worth the effort.

Mrs. Malcome was still grumbling. "I could have called about the flowers. You'll be late to school."

"Not if I hurry," Ruth Ann said. She caught up her books from the table and tucked her jacket under one arm. "I'll be home as soon as I can, and please don't frost the cake, Mrs. Malcome. I want to do it."

"The pleasure is all yours," Mrs. Malcome assured her. "You'd better wear your jacket. It's still a little nippy."

Ruth Ann hurried home as soon as school was out, but when she peeked in the garage her father's car wasn't parked in the usual place. Mrs. Malcome rose heavily from her place in front of the television screen and volunteered the information that they hadn't called.

"Oh well, maybe they didn't leave as early as they expected," Ruth Ann said. "Good. Now I'll have time to rearrange those flowers and get the cake iced." She changed her clothes, and then went into the kitchen and started to make the icing. Mrs. Malcome followed her and fussed around with dinner preparations, but obviously her heart wasn't in it.

"Can't imagine what happened to those two," she murmured once. "You sure your father said a little after noon?"

"That's what I understood. Of course, I could have made a mistake or they could have changed their minds or stopped somewhere along the way. They might have had some trouble with the car or run out of gas."

She ticked off the reasons easily, not really concerned. It wasn't even four o'clock, and they knew she usually didn't get home from school until around four.

But Mrs. Malcome was eyeing the clock unhappily. "I was sure they'd be here by now. Guess I'd better call Gracey and tell her I won't be able to come for dinner tonight."

"I don't see why you shouldn't go ahead," Ruth Ann said at once. "My goodness, it isn't every day that you're invited to a birthday party."

"Well, of course, Alfy had his *party* this afternoon," Mrs. Malcome explained. "This is just his birthday dinner. Gracey invites the whole family, and I'm always included because I'm his godmother. If it was one of the other children, I wouldn't mind, but Alfy's different. He was just a tiny baby when I first started to work there, so I feel that he's part mine. And he thinks the world and all of me, Alfy does . . . he'd be real sorry if I missed his birthday."

"You *can't* miss it," Ruth Ann said firmly. "You go right along and don't worry about a thing. I'll finish my cake and watch TV until they get here. You'll see them when you come on Monday."

Mrs. Malcome nodded, relieved. "I'll start to get ready then. They may even be here before I leave."

When Mrs. Malcome had gone and the beautifully iced cake was adorning the best cake plate on the sideboard, Ruth Ann went into her room and changed into a dress her father especially liked. She took a lot of time with her hair, too, and applied a touch of rosy lipstick.

It was five, and then five thirty, and then almost six. It was strange that her father hadn't called if they were delayed. He was thoughtful about things like that. But the car might have broken down in the middle of the desert. . . . Had he really said *noon?* Possibly the connection had been bad, and she had misunderstood the time.

When the telephone rang she leaped to answer it, but it was only Jeanie wanting to talk. Ruth Ann told her that she was expecting an important call; her father was late and might be trying to reach her this very minute. Jeanie said to call back when she had a chance.

The next time the telephone rang it was Mrs. Malcome, and she seemed disturbed when Ruth Ann admitted that they hadn't arrived.

"I'm not a bit worried, though," Ruth Ann assured her. "The more I think about it the more I think he said Friday *evening*. After all, it's a six-hour drive. It isn't reasonable that they'd get up at the crack of dawn to drive here by noon. Maybe he said they'd leave at noon, and then something happened to delay them."

She managed to convince Mrs. Malcome, but she

didn't succeed in convincing herself. Her father had said noon—sometime after noon.

Ruth Ann didn't look at the clock after that; she just sat and waited. Once she picked up the telephone gingerly, to be sure that it wasn't out of order, and replaced it when she heard the dial tone.

It was almost eight when someone rang the doorbell. Her father wouldn't ring; he had a key. Even Tracy had a key to the apartment.

She got to her feet, her heart hammering, and went to the door. Remembering, she did not open it until she put on the night latch. When she peered out and saw Mr. Conners standing in the hallway, she felt a quick surge of relief.

Quickly she unlatched the door and held it open. "Oh, Mr. Conners, didn't you know? Dad isn't here yet. They went to Palm Springs on their honeymoon, but I'm expecting. . . ." Her voice dwindled off into silence as he came into the apartment and closed the door behind him.

She had known Mr. Conners for years, since she was about eight years old. Mr. Conners and her father golfed together and sometimes bowled together. They visited at each other's homes, and Mrs. Conners and Ruth's mother used to play bridge together a long time ago. There was absolutely no reason, now, to be terrified. But she was terrified.

Mr. Conners took off his hat, pushed his hand

95

back across his thinning brown hair, and spoke gently. "I'm sorry, Ruth Ann. There's been an accident. I had a call from the state patrol, and I told them I'd bring you as soon as possible." He glanced past her. "You aren't alone, are you?"

"I sent Mrs. Malcome to a dinner party," she heard herself answer. Then she added carefully, "It was Alfy's birthday."

"We can talk on the way," he said. "It's quite a long drive. You'll need a coat, I think."

Ruth Ann went into her room obediently and got her coat. She even remembered to click off all the lights and to check that her keys were in her handbag, but she went through the motions automatically like a puppet.

In the car, driving toward the strange town he had mentioned, she forced herself to ask, "Is it very bad, Mr. Conners?"

"I'm afraid so. They are both listed as critical."

"But not. . . . He isn't dead?" The question sounded stupid and unreasonable. She knew her father couldn't be dead, but she had to hear Mr. Conners say so.

"No," he said, and Ruth Ann felt her knees go weak with relief and a surging gratitude.

"Is Tracy badly hurt?" she asked belatedly.

"I didn't talk to the doctor. I tried to reach him at the hospital as soon as I heard, but I wasn't able to

96

get in touch with him." Mr. Conners spoke without taking his eyes from the road. "Evidently the car plunged over an embankment, and it was some time before they could free them. Your father had me listed as the one to reach in case of an accident. Did you know about that, Ruth Ann?"

She shook her head. She hadn't known, but it was like her father to have thought of doing so. He wouldn't want a stranger to call her with such shocking news, and naturally he would think of Mr. Conners instead of Mrs. Malcome, who was inclined to go all to pieces in an emergency, or Dr. Melburn, who always seemed to be unavailable when you were in a hurry.

"We're almost there," Mr. Conners said, when she was convinced that the nightmare ride would go on forever. "Don't be alarmed if they don't let you see your father right away. These things take time."

He didn't explain what he meant by "these things," but Ruth Ann supposed he was referring to X rays and bandages and setting broken bones. "Do they know how long ago it happened?" she asked, and Mr. Conners shook his head.

"I really don't know, Ruth Ann. They called me at four or shortly after. I didn't want to tell you until I had things settled—whether you could see them and whether the hospital staff thought it advisable. I believe the nurse said they were brought in around two

97

o'clock, but of course it took some time for the wrecker and the ambulance crew to get them out of the car."

He parked in the hospital parking lot and came around to open the door for Ruth Ann.

The hospital wasn't very big—nothing like the one where her father had met Tracy—but all the lights burned bright, and there were a lot of cars and people coming and going. Ruth Ann looked up and saw a window blooming with plants on the second floor. When I come back tomorrow, she thought clearly, I must remember to bring flowers.

FIVE

"Is this the daughter?" the woman at the reception desk asked, her eyes sweeping over Ruth Ann and coming back to Mr. Conners.

Mr. Conners was wonderful. He answered questions and filled out all the papers that were pushed across the desk toward him. He made Ruth Ann sit down in one of the comfortable chairs in the lobby, but she sat tensely, her shoulders hunched forward so that she could hear better.

Visiting hours were over and people kept spilling out of the elevators and going in all directions. Some of the faces were tight and worried, but quite a few were smiling, and one rude little boy whispered behind his hand and giggled as he passed the chair in which Ruth Ann was sitting. The mother looked embarrassed as she took the child's hand and jerked him along after her. Ruth Ann wished, wearily, that she could let the woman know that it didn't matter. She didn't really care if the boy thought she was fat and funny looking.

99

Mr. Conners came over, sat down, and asked if she'd like a cup of tea or coffee while she waited. "The nurse says there's a good snack bar in the basement."

Ruth Ann shook her head. "No, thank you. I really don't care for anything."

Mr. Conners picked up a magazine and leafed through it, frowning. After a moment he put it aside and said he thought he'd catch a quick cup of coffee if she didn't mind.

Still Ruth Ann sat there, not wanting to look at a magazine or watch the TV set or even *think*. If she kept her mind a complete blank she might not be so scared. If she could think of something that had nothing to do with her father . . . something like the geometry tests that were looming at the end of the term. She closed her eyes and tried to picture the formulas in her mind. Her father had taught her that this way was the best. If one could *see* a problem in his mind's eye . . . all the angles and squares and sides. . . .

Her throat ached with tears, but she kept swallowing them. When they let her see her father she didn't want to look like a freshly boiled lobster. Some girls looked pretty when they cried, but not Ruth Ann. She knew what she looked like . . . like a big blubbering crybaby.

A young nurse came down the corridor that

stretched back from the lobby. She was smiling and her crisp white cap was perky instead of sedate. When she stopped at the desk to speak to the woman on duty, she stood on tiptoe and leaned forward with her weight balanced on the palms of her hands, like a dancer. They talked for a moment, and then the older woman laughed and shook her head, and they murmured some more. It seemed strange that they should be so carefree and unconcerned in a place like this—a place where people were ill, were in pain, were even dying. Yet the receptionist had seemed kind, and the young nurse was probably a perfectly normal girl who cried at sad movies and bit her fingernails when she was nervous. Facing tragedy was her job, something that went on day after day, night after night. Maybe she didn't even like being a nurse very much. Maybe she was waiting for a patient to fall in love with her and want to marry her and take her away from the hospital. Or perhaps she would marry a doctor. Tracy said that young nurses often married doctors.

She thought of Mrs. Malcome, but there was no way to get in touch with her. It was too bad, because if Mrs. Malcome called the apartment and got no answer she would be terribly upset.

Mr. Conners came back, and when she mentioned Mrs. Malcome he said that he would get in touch with the manager of the apartment house. If Mrs.

Malcome was really concerned, she'd get in touch with him.

A long time later a doctor came down in the elevator and walked over to the desk. He lighted a cigarette and talked to the nurse for a moment before he came over to speak to Ruth and Mr. Conners. "I'm Dr. Fredericks," he said, extending his hand to Mr. Conners and giving Ruth Ann a brief mechanical smile. "I expect Miss Callahan is anxious to see her father and . . . stepmother, isn't it?"

Nodding, she got to her feet feeling more awkward than ever. She towered over Dr. Fredericks, who was a small man. He didn't seem to be in any hurry to take her to her father, and he talked to Mr. Conners briefly before crushing out his cigarette in a convenient ashtray.

"I'll have to ask you to keep your visit short. A couple of minutes," he told her. "Try not to cry or to say anything that will upset him. And don't be disturbed if he's unconscious. We've given him a lot of sedation, and it may have taken effect by now. This way please. . . ."

He led her back to the elevator and jabbed the button for the third floor. There was another doctor in the car, and the two men talked about a baseball game. When they reached the third floor, Dr. Fredericks held the door open while he finished the conversation. It was annoying but oddly reassuring at

102

the same time. If her father were dying, the doctor certainly wouldn't be standing there talking about a ball game.

He led her down the corridor and stopped before a closed door. "Two minutes," Dr. Fredricks reminded her. He opened the door and stepped aside to let her enter.

The room was small, that was the first thing she noticed. It was hard to believe that the motionless figure on the high bed was her father. There were so many bandages that she couldn't be sure. She tiptoed closer and saw that a bottle upended beside the bed was attached to a tube in his arm. There was absolutely no color in his face—what she could see of his face—but when she stopped beside the bed his eyes opened, and they were her father's eyes, filled with love and worry and a vast tenderness.

"Hello, Daddy." She leaned over and kissed his cheek softly. "Don't try to talk. It's probably very bad for you. I . . . I just wanted to see you for a moment before Mr. Conners takes me home."

His voice was faint, but a smile flickered across his face. "It was some way to wind up a honeymoon, wasn't it?"

"Just so you're both O.K.," Ruth Ann said. "That's all that matters."

"Have you seen Tracy?"

"I wanted to see you first," Ruth Ann said with

103

perfect truth. "Now I'll be able to tell her that you're getting along fine."

He tried to smile, but she could see it was an effort. She put her hand against his cheek and spoke as firmly as she could manage. "Try to get some rest, that's the important thing, and don't *worry*. Everything will be fine. O.K.?"

His eyes closed wearily, and then opened again. "O.K.," he said. "Good night, honey." She put her face down against his, and when she straightened up she thought he was already asleep. Then, as she started to move backward toward the door, his voice stopped her. "Kiss Tracy good-night for me. Tell her I'm sorry." He still didn't open his eyes.

Dr. Fredericks, who had been waiting just inside the door, motioned her out of the room. "He'll sleep now," he said, when they were in the corridor. "He's been fighting the sedation until he could see you."

He led her farther along the corridor and stopped before another door that had a *No Visitors* sign hanging from the knob. "Don't stay long," he warned her again. "Mrs. Callahan has been in shock. She may be a little incoherent."

Mrs. Callahan. It was strange to think of Tracy as Mrs. Callahan.

A nurse was fussing over Tracy's bed when Ruth Ann came in. She indicated a chair near the window, and Ruth Ann went over and sat down quietly.

Tracy's eyes were closed and her arm was in a cast. One cheek was heavily bandaged, and the room was heavy with the cloying odor of an anesthetic. Tracy didn't look poised and slim and all the other things that Ruth had envied in her. She looked defense-less.

The nurse straightened up and nodded at Ruth as she unwound a rubber strap from Tracy's arm. "Well, that's all for this time, Mrs. Callahan," she said in the bright voice that nurses habitually reserve for the sickroom. "I'll let you visit for five minutes—no more—and then you get a hypo whether you want one or not." She spanked the bedspread smartly and bustled off.

Ruth Ann moved to the side of the bed. "Tracy. . . ." She whispered the name and at once Tracy's eyes opened and stared at her. Ruth felt as if she were looking into the eyes of a department-store dummy. There was no sign of life or recognition. "Tracy, it's me. It's Ruth Ann."

"Me. . . ." Tracy framed the word carefully with her pale lips. "Hello, *me*. I just had a wonderful dream. I dreamed I got rid of you." She closed her eyes again.

Ruth Ann swallowed. The doctor had warned her that Tracy might not be rational. Without opening her eyes Tracy was going on in the same expression-less voice.

"It was such a beautiful dream. Robert was in the dream. Do you remember Robert?"

"Yes," Ruth Ann said, "He's my father."

"We don't have a father," Tracy said, and she sounded a little impatient. "There's just mother, only she died. She died a little bit every day, and finally there was nothing left. Not even one happy memory." She was still for a moment, and then went on in the same singsong voice. "People shouldn't cling to life like that. When the time comes they ought to be able to open their hands and let it go."

Ruth Ann looked around for the buzzer to summon the nurse, but she couldn't see anything and she was afraid to leave.

Tears were sliding along Tracy's cheeks, and she tried to move her arm, the one in the cast. "I don't want to open my hands and let it go. I want the dream to go on just a little longer." Her voice rose slightly and she opened her eyes, staring at Ruth as if she hated her. "Why don't you go away and leave me alone? Please go away. Just *go away!*"

The nurse came back and made soothing noises as she gave Tracy a hypodermic injection. Then she held her hand on Tracy's forehead and looked up at Ruth Ann. "I'm sorry," she said. "You'll have to leave."

Ruth Ann hesitated, and then leaned over and

kissed Tracy's damp cheek. "Robert said to kiss you good-night and tell you he was sorry. Good night, Tracy."

Her own cheeks were wet when she went out blindly into the corridor, but she dashed the tears away with the back of her hand. In a moment Dr. Fredericks appeared, and she followed him to the lobby where Mr. Conners was waiting.

Mr. Conners had fallen asleep with his head dropped forward on his chest, but he roused as soon as he heard their footsteps. Once again he took charge of the situation. He found out that Ruth Ann could come back at noon the following day and stay as long as she liked. Dr. Fredericks told them of a residence hall nearby where she might be able to get a room if the trip back and forth proved too inconvenient.

"We won't worry about that right now," Mr. Conners said. "I'll bring her tomorrow and we can make arrangements after that. The important thing is to get this girl home before she folds up."

Dr. Fredericks was looking at her soberly. "Would you like to have me give you something to help you sleep?"

"Oh no, no thank you," she said politely. "I mean, I won't have any trouble getting to sleep now that I know they're going to be all right." She might have imagined it, but she thought his eyes flickered a little when she said that. Pushing down the uneasiness, she thanked him again for being so kind.

When they were in the car driving back, Mr. Conners said that he and his wife would be happy to have Ruth Ann stay with them for a few days, until she could make other arrangements. He pointed out that she certainly wouldn't want to stay in the apartment by herself. Ruth Ann assured him that she be fine at the apartment and that the first thing in the morning she would call Mrs. Malcome.

He insisted on parking the car and coming upstairs with her, and she could see that he didn't like the idea of leaving her there by herself. "I'll lock up as soon as you leave and get right to bed," Ruth Ann said. "Thank you again, Mr. Conners, and I'll see you tomorrow."

"It may be eleven thirty before I can get here," he said. "I have to check in at the office first."

"I'll be ready whenever you come."

When she had locked up after Mr. Conners she was surprised to see that it wasn't yet midnight. It seemed to Ruth Ann that it had been a hundred years since she had opened the door and seen Mr. Conners standing there.

The flower arrangement was as fresh and lovely as it had been early in the day, and the three-tiered wedding cake that she had taken such pains with stood proudly on the sideboard. She went all through the apartment turning on the lights. She even turned on the light in her father's room, and her eyes smarted when she saw the nosegay of violets on the dressing table. Tomorrow when she went to the hospital she must remember to take the flowers.

The kitchen was sparkling clean. It was a shame to mar it with even an empty glass. When she finished a tall glass of milk, she rinsed and dried the glass, putting it back in the cupboard.

I ought to be starved, she reminded herself. I *am* starved, but I still don't want to eat. All my life— well, anyway for the last few years—I've wanted a reason for not eating, and now I have one. I'm punishing myself, that's what I'm doing. Punishing myself for hating Tracy and wanting her to go away. If I hadn't been so unpleasant about it, they'd have been married weeks ago, maybe even months ago, and this might never have happened.

She knew that she wasn't making much sense, but it was a relief to let the tears stream down her cheeks, to be able to sob into the cushion on the davenport until it was so damp that she had to turn it over and cry on the other side.

The doorbell rang startling her so that she sat up and stopped crying. The ring was repeated while she sat there, and she heard someone unlock the door and then Mrs. Malcome's worried voice. "Ruth Ann, you'll have to unlatch the door. My key doesn't work when you have the night latch on."

Slowly and wearily Ruth Ann got to her feet and

crossed the room. She slipped the chain out of the slot, and the door swung open. Almost at once she was enveloped in Mrs. Malcome's warm and somewhat damp embrace.

"You poor lamb," Mrs. Malcome said. "I've been so sorry and upset about leaving you. I'll never forgive myself that you had to be alone when you heard the terrible news . . . never!"

Behind Mrs. Malcome stood a middle-aged man who looked sorry and a little embarrassed. "I wanted to be sure you were here," he told Ruth Ann across Mrs. Malcome's shoulder. "We called the hospital, but couldn't get much information. Aunt Martha was sure you'd come back to the apartment, so we drove over."

"It was very kind of you to come," Ruth Ann said, "but it really wasn't necessary. I'll be perfectly all right, and in the morning Mr. Conners is coming to take me back to the hospital."

"I'm staying right here with you," Mrs. Malcome told her firmly. "I've been calling all evening and finally I got in touch with Mr. Peterson, and he told me about the accident. He said that some man had called from the hospital and that you were there. Finally I was so nervous that I made Kenny drive me over. I knew you'd be back sooner or later." Mrs. Malcome's several chins were trembling, and she looked as if she might burst into tears at any moment. "Kenny, will you stop and have a cup of tea with us? I'm sure this poor child could use one."

"No, no, if there's nothing I can do to help I'd better be getting back home," he said hastily. And then to Ruth Ann he added, "I hope they're going to be all right."

"I'm sure they will," she said steadily. "They let me go in and talk to both of them. I think that's a good sign, don't you?"

"A very good sign," he agreed. "Well, Aunt Martha, you know where to get in touch with me if you need a chauffeur. Take it easy now and don't sit up all night talking. You'll both need your sleep."

"Thank Gracey for the lovely dinner," Mrs. Malcome told him. "I was so upset I don't think I even thanked her properly."

Ruth Ann almost hated to see him leave. She told herself that she couldn't bear to listen to another of Mrs. Malcome's uninspired monologues tonight.

But Mrs. Malcome surprised her. She locked up after Kenny had gone, and then started resolutely around the apartment clicking off all the lights. "He's absolutely right, you know. You have to get some sleep if you don't want to look like the wrath of God when your father sees you tomorrow. How about that cup of tea? It might help you to get to sleep and calm you down a little." She had picked up the davenport cushion, but she didn't say anything

111

about it being damp. Instead, she smoothed it and put it back in its place.

"I really don't care for tea," Ruth Ann said. "I had a glass of milk a little while ago. I think I'll take an aspirin and go to bed."

"A good idea," Mrs. Malcome said. And then she added gently, "They did let you see your father? You were able to talk to him?"

"Yes. He was a little groggy, of course. The doctor said he'd been fighting the sedation until I got there." Her voice sounded a little stiff, like that of a child reciting a lesson it had learned too well. "Tracy, Tracy didn't know me. At least I hope she didn't know me. She told me to go away."

"Ahhh, the poor thing was probably in a lot of pain."

"No, it wasn't that. She looked at me as if . . . as if I were someone she *should* remember but would rather not."

Mrs. Malcome made a sympathetic clucking sound. "Now, now, Ruth Ann. Don't start imagining things. When this is all over and they are both home and well, you'll laugh about this. See if you don't."

"I hope so," Ruth Ann said. "Oh, Mrs. Malcome, I hope so."

She was certain she wouldn't be able to close her eyes, but almost as soon as her head touched the pillow she fell into a deep dreamless sleep.

112

The next morning Mrs. Malcome was bustling around in the kitchen humming under her breath. When she was happy Mrs. Malcome hummed happy tunes, old things like "Put on Your Old Gray Bonnet," or "In My Merry Oldsmobile," but when she was in a sober frame of mind she hummed church hymns. For a second Ruth Ann was able to believe that the events of the previous evening had been a nightmare, something she could shake off with the cold light of morning. She sat up and looked around and remembered. And fear was a knot in her stomach and an ache in her throat as she got dressed and ready for school.

Mrs. Malcome was surprised when she announced that as long as Mr. Conners wasn't coming until eleven thirty she might as well check in at school and get her assignments.

"But, Ruth Ann, it's Saturday. There's no school today," Mrs. Malcome said with unexpected gentleness.

It was the first time Ruth Ann could remember making such a stupid mistake. Saturday . . . but she had always looked forward to the weekend. She especially liked Friday, because it meant that the two-day holiday would soon begin. For two whole days she could putter around the apartment, visit with her father, make the things he liked to eat, and catch up on her reading. She didn't have to leave the

113

apartment except to go to church or perhaps take a ride with her father. No one looked at her and grinned and made unfunny remarks. Not that she ever admitted she was such a stay-at-home because she hated to have people look at her. Even the Saturday matinees with Jeanie were a trial. Her father never even suspected that the reason she went to early church was because fewer people attended then; he believed her when she said she went early so the day would be longer.

"Well, don't look so glum," Mrs. Malcome said. "As long as you're dressed you can run down to the creamery and get another quart of milk."

"Skim?" Ruth Ann asked, and Mrs. Malcome gave her a sharp look.

"It's up to you, missy. You're the one who always complains that it tastes like chalk."

"It does taste like chalk," Ruth Ann said. "But it's supposed to have as many vitamins as regular milk so I'll get it anyway."

She got her sweater, tied a scarf over her head, and went to the creamery for the milk. As long as she kept busy she wouldn't think about her father. She wouldn't think about Tracy looking at her with blank eyes, telling her to go away, begging her to go away and leave her alone.

She had turned and started back toward the apartment when she became aware that someone had rushed past her and then skidded to a stop. When she heard her name called, she turned her head. "Ruth Ann, hey, I was sorry to hear about your dad and his wife. I hope everything is going to be all right." It was Tony Barretto. She hadn't even realized that he lived around here.

"I haven't heard from the hospital this morning," she said. "I'm going over in a little while." And then, because she couldn't help it, she asked, "How did you hear about the accident?"

"It was on the late news," Tony told her. "I just happened to be listening to it and the name clicked right away. Some of the kids at school had mentioned your dad was getting married again, so when the fellow on TV said that this couple was returning from their honeymoon, I figured it had to be your dad."

"They were married just a week ago," Ruth Ann said. "They were supposed to be home yesterday, and then I heard. . . . My father's lawyer came and told me about the accident and took me over there to see them."

Tony's dark eyes were warm with sympathy. "That's tough, Ruth Ann. I'm sure sorry. If there's anything I can do, let me know. O.K.?"

She thanked him and moved on again, but she held his words close to her heart for comfort, even though she knew the remark was a conventional thing for him to say. It didn't have to mean anything, but she couldn't help hoping that it *did* mean something. Anyway, he had known that her name was Callahan and that her father had just been married.

She let herself into the apartment and found Mr. Conners waiting. He was sitting on the edge of the davenport holding his hat in his hands, as if no one had invited him to put it down.

"Oh, I'm sorry," she said at once. "I wasn't expecting you quite so soon, but I can be ready in two minutes. Why don't you let Mrs. Malcome give you a cup of coffee while. . . ."

He didn't answer and he didn't smile. He just sat there, and Ruth Ann felt a terrible urgency to go on talking and talking. "Did Mrs. Malcome tell you? I forgot all about it being Saturday and I got ready to go to school. Did you ever hear of anything so stupid?" She was looking around for Mrs. Malcome as she spoke. Normally Mrs. Malcome would be sitting right there talking his ear off. "Let me get you a cup of coffee. I'll pick up the flowers I want to take to Tracy. . . ."

"Ruth Ann," he interrupted her softly. "Please sit down and listen to me for a minute."

"Oh, no." She felt as if she were shouting the words, although her lips moved soundlessly. "No, no, no!"

116

She heard a dry sob from the doorway and turned her head to see Mrs. Malcome's face contorted with weeping. Ruth Ann looked back at Mr. Conners. "My father?" she whispered.

"Yes. I'm sorry, Ruth Ann. It must have happened soon after we left the hospital. The doctor said he seemed to hold on just long enough to see you again."

She sat down on the nearest chair, still holding the quart of milk as carefully as if it had been filled with diamonds. If she moved too suddenly she had the feeling that she would start to fall apart, to crumble. She closed her eyes and took half-a-dozen long painful breaths. From a long way off she could hear Mr. Conners' voice going on and on and on.

"I'll come back later in the day," she heard that much. "There are certain arrangements that have to be made, but if you would prefer that I take care of them. . . ."

"Arrangements?"

"Your father was a very thoughtful man, Ruth Ann. There will be very little for you to do. Of course, his marriage complicates things somewhat."

Ruth Ann opened her eyes and looked at him. "What about Tracy?"

He shook his head. "Still critical. They had to tell her, of course."

Ruth Ann nodded. "Of course."

117

Strangely, even in that first numbing grief, she could be sorry for Tracy. Ruth Ann had known her father and loved him for sixteen years; he had belonged to Tracy for only seven days.

SIX

Afterward Ruth Ann was glad that she had only the dimmest memory of the days that followed.

She didn't return to school on Monday.

Mr. Conners was wonderfully efficient about making all the necessary arrangements, and he repeated his invitation to Ruth Ann to come and stay with them until things had been straightened out. But Ruth Ann preferred to stay on at the apartment with Mrs. Malcome. Only now Mrs. Malcome stayed all the time instead of coming in daily.

Later, Mr. Conners told her, they would all sit down and have a long talk about what should be done, but at first it was easier to drift, to move about the familiar rooms and pretend that it was all a bad dream, that at any moment she might awaken and hear her father's key in the lock, her father's voice calling her name. One night—the night before the funeral—she wakened from a restless sleep and sat bolt upright in bed, thinking she had heard him say her name. But even as she stumbled along the hall-

119

way in the darkness and pushed open the door to his room, she knew that she wouldn't find him there, that he was gone.

Mrs. Malcome heard her and came out of her room, belting her bathrobe briskly and speaking in the firm tone she had adopted to mask her sympathy. "Come now," she said. "Let me get you a glass of warm milk. It'll help you get back to sleep." But in spite of her briskness her eyes were full of pity.

Ruth Ann followed Mrs. Malcome into the brightness of the kitchen and accepted the warm milk docilely enough. It was hard to swallow, but Mrs. Malcome was watching so she drained the glass down to the last drop.

"I'm sorry I woke you," she said. "I must have been asleep and I thought . . . I thought I heard Father calling."

Mrs. Malcome nodded. "I know, dear." She sounded as if she really did know. Perhaps after Mr. Malcome died she, too, had awakened in the night thinking that he had called her name.

And Mrs. Malcome had been left alone, too. Completely alone, just as Ruth Ann was alone.

"It's funny, isn't it?" she heard herself saying. "Most people have families—not always brothers and sisters, but at least cousins and aunts and uncles —someone to belong to. But you didn't have anyone either after Mr. Malcome died."

120

Mrs. Malcome was watching her and trying hard not to yawn in her face. Poor Mrs. Malcome, the past days had been hard on her, too. "That's right," she said. "But you aren't alone, Ruth Ann. You still have Tracy."

Ruth Ann shook her head. "No," she said, "Tracy and I never really liked one another. We hardly knew each other. We might have learned to be friends, because of Father, because we both loved him and wanted him to be happy, but now there isn't anything to hold us together."

"That's a pity," Mrs. Malcome said. "Because now you'll both be lonely."

When she went back to bed Ruth Ann kept remembering Mrs. Malcome's words. "Now you'll both be lonely."

But the situation would be different for Tracy. Tracy could simply move back to the life she had left so recently. She had her work, her friends at the hospital, and her house. She had been delighted at the idea of a house of her own after all the years of living in apartments and other people's houses.

Ruth Ann turned her pillow and put her face down against it. She didn't really wish that Tracy had died instead of her father. She wasn't wicked enough to wish that.

She had seen Tracy only once since that night at the hospital. Mr. Conners had suggested that they drive over and consult with her about the arrangements he had made. The visit was a strange one, but then . . . they were still almost strangers. They had nothing in common but the man who had loved both of them.

Tracy would be in the hospital for some time. There could be no question of her attending the funeral, the doctors said. When she was stronger she would be moved to the hospital where she had worked for so long, where she had so many friends. The convalescence would probably be much easier for Tracy when she was among the people she knew.

Tracy was more like her old self—quiet and self-contained. She said all the correct sympathetic words, but she didn't cry and her face was carefully blank when Mr. Conners told her of the arrangements.

"I'm sure you've handled everything beautifully, Mr. Conners. I'm sure Robert would approve. Thank you for looking out for Ruth Ann." She might easily have been talking about the stocks and bonds and insurance policies that had been discussed.

There had been just one moment when Tracy seemed to come alive, to look back and remember and be sorry. It came as Ruth was leaving, when she had already turned toward the door.

"Ruth?" There had been a strange forlorn note in

her voice, a note almost of pleading, but when Ruth turned back Tracy's face was expressionless again.

"Yes?" Ruth Ann came back to the bedside and looked down at Tracy. All of a sudden she remembered that this loss was Tracy's as well as her own, but there were no words to bring the sudden feeling of kinship out into the open. She could only stand there, miserable and awkward and tongue-tied.

After a long moment Tracy made a small movement with her free hand, as if she wanted to comfort herself by reaching for Ruth's, but then she turned her face away and her hand was limp and quiet against the white spread.

"When you came to see me the other day," she said quietly, "I thought I'd dreamed it, but the nurse says you were here and that I told you to go away." Her eyes turned back to Ruth Ann's face. "I'm sorry. It was thoughtful of you to come and see me. I know you must have been deeply troubled about your father, but you came and I made you cry. The nurse said you were crying when you left."

"It doesn't matter," Ruth Ann said. "You weren't yourself; you'd had a lot of medication."

They were being scrupulously polite, and the politeness was like a shield or a wall. They could talk over it, but they couldn't reach one another.

There wasn't another opportunity to go to the hospital and visit Tracy. First was the matter of the funeral. Somehow from somewhere she had to find the strength to get through her father's funeral.

Mrs. Malcome took care of the details like deciding what Ruth Ann should wear, as if it made any difference what she wore. Who would see her? Who would even notice?

Her father knew a great many people and so did Tracy. A lot of them were at the funeral. They came up to Ruth Ann and murmured words of sympathy and moved off again, but the faces were a blur and the voices just a murmuring background for the feeling of emptiness and loss. The funeral director gave her a large envelope filled with the cards that had been on the floral pieces, and a box of cards and envelopes. Mrs. Malcome explained that she was supposed to send thank-you cards.

"Why?" Ruth Ann asked, and for once Mrs. Malcome was speechless.

At last the funeral service and the prayers were over. Ruth Ann sat stiffly upright beside Mrs. Malcome at the funeral home and let Mr. Conners take her arm as they followed the six men carrying the bronze box to its final resting place in the cemetery plot. She had the strangest feeling that she had lived through all of this in another life, and then she remembered that it wasn't another life at all. She was remembering four years ago when her mother died. Only then she had walked beside her father and his hand holding hers had given her strength and comfort.

It was over and she was home again. Only now the apartment didn't seem like home. Mr. Conners suggested that she drop the lease on the apartment when it terminated early in the summer. He talked about a summer camp or a dude ranch for the vacation months. It would be good for her, he said with assurance, to get into a new environment, meet new people, make new friends. When it was time for school again, she could go to some good girl's school. Mrs. Conners was making inquiries. There wasn't any hurry, of course. Mrs. Malcome agreed to stay on for a time.

Ruth Ann listened and neither agreed nor disagreed. These matters just weren't that important. She liked Mr. and Mrs. Conners, and she knew that they were doing their best to fulfill their responsibilities, but she couldn't help wishing that they would go away and forget about her.

She started back to school and people were kind. At first they were so kind that it was a little embarrassing. She had never been a friendly girl, and no one except Jeanie had made a point of singling her out of the mob, so now when the teachers expressed their sympathy or any of the others told her how sorry they were she didn't know how to respond.

Jeanie hadn't been around much since the accident. Ruth Ann knew it was because she didn't know what to say. She wondered why Jeanie should feel awkward with a girl she had known for so many years. Why couldn't she just say that she was sorry, or something equally simple? Instead, Jeanie avoided the subject and pretended that it wasn't there. And yet, in Jeanie's shoes she'd probably behave the same way.

Ruth Ann got through those first two days at school, and on the surface everything was back to normal. The old comradeship with Jeanie was picked up as easily as it had been dropped. Jeanie still didn't care about coming to the apartment, though, because of Mrs. Malcome. ". . . because honestly, Ruth Ann, you have to admit that she's the biggest bore since the year one. Always talking about the old days and people you never even met. And giving advice that no one is remotely interested in."

Ruth Ann nodded and swallowed the lump that always seemed to be stuck in her throat these days. "I know, but she's been a good friend to me, Jeanie. I honestly don't think I'd have managed without her these past weeks."

Jeanie scowled. "Well, my goodness, Ruth Ann, it isn't all *that* long! It's just been a week since the accident."

A week. Jeanie was right, of course. It was Friday again, but it seemed months and months since that

126

day when she had rushed home from school to rear-range the flowers and ice the welcome-home cake.

The flowers had died and been thrown out, but the three-tiered cake was in a sealed box in the freezer. Mrs. Malcome had taken care of it.

That same night Mr. and Mrs. Conners came to see her. They called before they came and tried to make it seem social, but Mr. Conners carried a brief-case that was stuffed with important-looking papers for her to sign. He told her that in his talks with Tracy they had made decisions about the insurance policies and paying the expenses and things like that. Everything had been taken care of.

"How is Tracy?" Ruth Ann asked. "I haven't heard since the day you drove me out there. I called the hospital once, but all the nurses have to say is that she's doing as well as can be expected."

Mr. Conners was suddenly very busy looking at the papers. "I'm afraid she isn't doing too well, Ruth Ann. She has regained almost complete use of her hands and arms, but the lower limbs are still para-lyzed."

Ruth Ann stared at him. "You mean she's crip-pled? She can't walk?"

He looked at his wife, as if for help, and then spoke soothingly. "Well, of course, everyone is hop-ing that this condition is temporary. Fortunately, Tracy has a remarkable constitution, and her medi-

127

cal background will help her to make the necessary adjustments. In many ways your father's wife is a remarkable young woman. She made it quite clear that she didn't want her condition to . . . in any way . . . affect the disposition of your father's estate."

"I don't understand what that means," Ruth Ann admitted bluntly. "I don't understand much about any of this, but if Tracy is crippled. . . ." She stopped, and then began again more calmly. "Did she know about this the day I was there?"

Mr. Conners looked bewildered. "I'm sure she did. The doctors wouldn't try to hide it from her, and certainly Tracy herself must have known right from the first." He shuffled some more papers around on the tabletop and cleared his throat. "It's important that you understand about your father's will, Ruth Ann. . . ."

He went on and on and on, but Ruth Ann scarcely listened, and when he finally stopped talking and looked to her for some comment, she merely asked the question she had been waiting to ask. "What is she going to do, Mr. Conners?"

He looked bewildered again, his mind still cluttered with facts and figures and legal terminology. It was his wife who answered Ruth Ann. She had been watching and listening, but taking no part in the conversation. Now she spoke gently. "She was planning to be moved back to her old hospital sometime this next week. She has some hospitalization plan that will take care of most of the expenses for a few months, but of course she doesn't expect to be in there too long. I got the impression that she hadn't made any long-range plans."

"Did she say anything about her house?" Ruth persisted.

"No. She didn't mention a house. I can't remember her talking about a house. Mostly she wanted to talk about you, what we were planning for you."

Ruth Ann looked back at Mr. Conners, who was busily checking all the places where she should sign the papers. "Could I go to see her again, Mr. Conners? I mean, I think I ought to talk to her."

"I'm sure she'd be delighted to see you," he said in the positive tone of someone who knew nothing of the sort. "Would you like to have me take you over on Sunday?"

She shook her head, and then picked up the pen and started signing the papers carefully. "No, thank you. I think I'd like to go by myself. Maybe I'll go tomorrow."

The next morning Mrs. Malcome offered to go with her, but Ruth Ann declined the company, so Mrs. Malcome went to spend the day at the zoo with Alfy, and Ruth Ann caught the bus that went through the town where the hospital was situated.

When she went to Tracy's room she found Tracy

129

propped up against the pillows. There was a magazine within easy reach, but she wasn't reading. She looked as if she might have been half-sitting, half-lying in the same position for hours. She wasn't even looking at anything . . . just waiting.

"Hello, Tracy," Ruth Ann said from the doorway. "I hope you're feeling better."

Tracy's clear eyes darkened a little, as if seeing Ruth Ann made her recall something she was trying to forget, and then almost at once she smiled. "Come in, Ruth," she said. "I've been thinking about you a lot. I intended to call you before now, but the phone booths in this place aren't built to accommodate wheelchairs, and the phone at the desk is always so noisy."

Ruth Ann tried not to glance at the telephone on the stand across the room, but Tracy must have noticed. "My own telephone isn't connected." She made a little face. "Some sort of therapy. If things are too easy for me, I won't make the effort, or anyway, that's what they tell me."

Ruth Ann's eyes slid past the wheelchair by the window and the plants that adorned the dresser and then back to Tracy's face. "I didn't know . . . about your legs," she said. "I'm very sorry." She sat down without being asked, and for the first time she didn't feel awkward and heavy under Tracy's watchful eyes.

"Well, of course, we have hopes that this thing is temporary." Tracy's tone dismissed the subject. "How about you, Ruth Ann? Are you getting along all right?"

"I'm fine. Mr. Conners is looking after things. Right now he's trying to decide what to do with me for the summer. I have dozens of folders about summer camps and dude ranches. And we're finding out about schools for next fall. Boarding schools...."

"I know." Tracy said.

"Mr. Conners thinks that before the lease expires on the apartment, we should have everything planned. Mrs. Malcome will be going to Canada to visit those friends of hers, but she says she'll stay as long as I need her."

Tracy's gray eyes were still watching her . . . waiting. . . .

Ruth Ann twisted her hands together and took a deep breath. "But I was thinking . . . I was thinking that if you haven't made any plans, if you haven't decided what you'll do when you're able to leave the hospital, we might stay together and see if we can work something out. Unless you'd rather not, of course."

For a long moment Tracy said nothing. Then her lips moved. "Why?" she asked.

Ruth Ann leaned forward earnestly. "Because we're both going to need someone. We're both going to be lonely. And I think Father would like us to be together, don't you?"

Tracy closed her eyes for a moment. "Yes," she said faintly, "I think he'd like that."

"I expect that legally you're my guardian, or anyway Mr. Conners could fix it up so that you'd be the one to decide about money and such things. I haven't had much experience in that line, but I'm really good at other things, Tracy. I really am. I'm a good cook and housekeeper, and I could do all the shopping and washing and things like that. Father used to say that I could iron his shirts better than the Chinese laundry."

Tracy turned her head away. Her voice was suddenly very tired. "Ruth Ann, are you offering to take care of me? Is that what you're saying?"

Ruth Ann started to say no, and then stopped herself. If she and Tracy were to make this arrangement work, they had to be completely honest with one another. "I guess right now I need someone to . . . to look after and belong to even more than you need to be taken care of. It's important to be necessary to someone—you said that yourself—but most of all I guess I'm afraid of being lonely." Tracy still didn't look at her so she went on. "The lease on the apartment isn't up until the first of June, that means we'd have most of April and all of May before we have to make any final decision. Your things are all at the apartment, so we wouldn't have that problem, and I

132

think Mr. Conners would be happy if he knew we were going to be together."

Tracy turned her head slowly. "You really have thought about it. Have you discussed it with Mr. Conners?"

"I wanted to talk to you first," Ruth Ann said. "If you thought it was a stupid idea, we could just drop it and . . . and Mr. Conners wouldn't have to know anything about it. It doesn't have to be forever, you know. If it doesn't work out, if you decide you aren't happy and want to call it off, well, I can still go to that dude ranch until it's time for school to start. If they can find a horse strong enough to lift me, that is." She tossed in the last remark just to lighten the moment, but Tracy didn't smile. "It doesn't have to be forever," she said again.

"That's right," Tracy said. "It doesn't have to be forever."

"So . . . so I hope you'll be thinking about it. You wouldn't have to say yes or no right away, but as soon as you can leave the hospital you could come home to the apartment. Mrs. Malcome will be there to look after you while I'm at school."

"Who needs Mrs. Malcome?" Tracy asked. "I get along fine in that contraption. You'll be surprised to see the way I can scoot around."

Ruth Ann looked at her soberly. "That sounds as if you might come."

Tracy smiled and held out her thin hand. Ruth

133

took it almost without thinking. "Now I will really try." Tracy whispered the words more to herself than to Ruth Ann. "Now that I have a reason I will really try to get better."

Ruth Ann looked down at their clasped hands— Tracy's so thin and capable and her own so square and plump.

Friendship is two people coming together from different directions with their hands outstretched. . . . She remembered Tracy saying that a long time ago. She couldn't help wondering if maybe Tracy remembered it, too.

SEVEN

Mr. Conners was delighted when Ruth told him of her visit with Tracy and of their decision. He was so delighted that he got a little emotional about it, taking off his glasses and polishing them furiously, and then leaning across the table to pat her hand. "That's fine, Ruth Ann. That's wonderful. I know your father would be very pleased."

Mrs. Malcome was emotional about it, too. She said she was proud of Ruth Ann and knew that her father, God rest him, was watching and was proud of her, too.

Their reaction was a little embarrassing, as if they were giving her credit for something she hadn't done. She wasn't being noble, for heaven's sake, and she had been completely honest when she told Tracy that she was afraid of loneliness, afraid of not being needed.

Jeanie made no secret of the fact that she thought Ruth Ann was out of her mind. "I think you're crazy, I really do, Ruth Ann. I think all this has unhinged you. You could have gone away to a summer camp or dude ranch and had a simply fabulous summer, and what do you do? Get tied up with an invalid who isn't even a relative of yours!"

"She's my stepmother, if we want to get technical," Ruth Ann reminded her.

"But you didn't even want your father to marry her. You nearly had a fit because he was going to."

"I guess I did," Ruth Ann said. "It all seems a long time ago."

Jeanie looked exasperated. "I still think it's stupid. You and Tracy will probably hate each other inside of a week, but you'll be stuck with her. I know you. You won't feel that you can go off and leave her by herself, so you'll be fetching and carrying all summer long."

Ruth Ann looked at her friend thoughtfully. She could see now what Mrs. Malcome meant when she said that Jeanie was a selfish little baggage, who would never care about anyone but herself. Mrs. Malcome declared that *she* could tell by the way Jeanie's eyes were set too close together and the little droop at the corners of her mouth.

Jeanie was looking crosser than ever. "Now what are you staring at me for?" she demanded.

"I was noticing your eyes," Ruth Ann said with a faint smile. Then she added, "They certainly are *brown*, almost a chocolate brown."

Jeanie looked pleased. Jeanie took almost any remark as a compliment.

On Monday Tracy was transferred by ambulance to the hospital in town. She said she didn't really need the ambulance, but as long as her insurance paid for it, why not?

"I expected to come down the highway ninety miles an hour, with sirens screaming," she told Ruth Ann over the phone. "But the driver said they only did that in case of emergency." Tracy sounded almost like her old self. She told Ruth she had a lovely room "right in the middle of everything" and that some of her friends were dropping in all day long.

"Don't get to liking it too much," Ruth Ann said. "You won't want to leave and come home." Strange, how easily she could say things to make Tracy feel wanted and missed, and the strangest part was that she meant every word. She did want Tracy to come home to the apartment.

Ruth Ann went to the hospital almost every day after school. The nurses came to know her, and there was no nonsense about waiting until visiting hours. Tracy could manage her wheelchair beautifully, but whenever Ruth Ann came she would let her push it.

"After all, I expect to be out of this contraption in a short time. There's no point in letting myself develop big bulging muscles," she told Ruth Ann gaily.

They went all over the hospital, and Tracy introduced Ruth Ann to the nurses and doctors and some
of the patients as Robert's daughter. Some of them
had known Robert when he was a patient.

Sometimes she and Tracy had long talks in the
quiet of Tracy's room. They found a lot to say. Tracy
called the conversations "catching up talk." Ruth
Ann told her about the years when she was growing
up, and she was able to talk about her father without
having her eyes fill with tears. Tracy talked about
him, too—the things that she remembered—but
Tracy never cried, not once.

Mrs. Malcome fussed a little, because Ruth spent
so much time at the hospital. "I declare, Ruth Ann,
you don't recognize a middle ground, do you? It has
to be all or nothing. Tracy will be coming home
soon, and you'll be able to spend years and years
together—until you grow up and get married, or
until she gets married again. There's no reason why
you should feel that you have to spend every waking
moment with her, is there?"

"Do you think I'm making a pest of myself?" Ruth
Ann asked. "Is that what you mean, Mrs. Malcome?"

Mrs. Malcome sniffed, and then relented. "No, of
course, I don't mean that. I'm sure you're a big comfort to Tracy. Because you want to be with her, she
has a family. You are a part of the man she married,
and so while she has you she hasn't entirely lost
him."

138

Mrs. Malcome had a talent for making things sound soggy and sentimental, but Ruth Ann knew that if Tracy *did* like her it wasn't for any such reason.

She thought about it, though. She thought about it a lot, and she had to admit finally that it was she who had changed, not Tracy. Tracy had always wanted to be her friend; she was the one who had turned her back. Yet now she was the one who made the gestures. Why? She couldn't honestly say that she had grown that fond of Tracy, but Tracy needed her. Tracy was ill. It might be years before she would be able to walk again. She might be in that wheelchair for the rest of her life.

Maybe Jeanie's right, and I do want someone to fetch and carry for, Ruth Ann thought. Maybe I'm using Tracy as an excuse for not getting out and making a life of my own. As long as I can believe that Tracy depends on me I won't have to think about all the years ahead, all the empty lonely years.

And then one day, when she was pushing Tracy around the hospital grounds and they had stopped to rest for a moment, Tracy said almost the same thing. She had been asking Ruth about what she was planning to do with the summer and Ruth answered, in some surprise, that she hadn't thought much about it. "We'll think of things to do. Dad and I used to go on little weekend jaunts, and sometimes when he went golfing I rode along and sat in the car and read or wrote letters." She smiled a little when she said that, and then hastened to explain. "I used to write twenty or thirty letters a week. I was a pen pal."

Tracy nodded. "That sounds interesting. What happened to your pen pals? I mean, you can't be a pen pal by yourself, can you?"

Ruth frowned. "I guess you outgrow being a pen pal. When girls are around twelve and thirteen, it's something to keep them busy, but by the time real life catches up with them. . . ." She paused and lifted her shoulders in a shrug. "Anyway, one by one they stopped writing."

Tracy was regarding her seriously. "What do you mean by 'real life' catching up with them?"

"Oh, you know." Ruth's tone was elaborately casual. "Dates and boyfriends and things like that."

"Did you ever meet any of your pen pals, Ruth?"

"Oh, no. I guess I always chose the ones who lived a long, long way away, so that there wouldn't be any chance of that happening. One girl did write that she was coming out once, but I told her some fib about having to go to visit an aunt or cousin." She looked at Tracy defensively. "I didn't actually pass myself off as a raving beauty in those pen-pal letters, but I never sent pictures or anything like that, either."

140

Tracy was silent for a moment, and then she spoke firmly. "Ruth, this was one of the things that Robert worried about . . . about you. He blamed himself because you were so involved in seeing to his comfort and looking after him that you didn't have time for the youngsters your own age."

"I haven't ever cared much for the youngsters my own age," Ruth Ann reminded her. "I guess I'm not very normal."

Tracy smiled, but the smile wasn't very convincing. "Normal or not, I can't let you use me for an excuse to push life away from you. You understand that, don't you?"

"I don't know what you mean," Ruth said.

"I think you do, or anyway you'd understand if you let yourself think about it. Ever since your mother died you tried to be the most important person in the world to your father. You'd have loved to have him completely dependent on you. And now you've lost your father and you need to transfer all that attention and devotion to someone else . . . to me." Tracy paused and waited, but Ruth said nothing. "If I wasn't in this wheelchair, Ruth, if I hadn't been hurt in the accident, would you still have wanted us to stay together and be a family?"

"Yes, of course," Ruth said unsteadily.

"Fine," Tracy said. "I'll hold you to that." She didn't explain further, and there was no reason why

141

the conversation should have left Ruth feeling so uneasy—no reason at all.

And then one day Ruth came home from school and let herself into the apartment as usual. She stopped just inside the door and lifted her head and listened. Usually she could see Mrs. Malcome sitting in her favorite chair watching television, but today she was nowhere in evidence. Someone was moving about in the kitchen, but it wasn't Mrs. Malcome; she was sure of that. As she waited she heard the clatter of a spoon in a bowl, and then the sliding shooshing sound that had become more and more familiar these past weeks.

Ruth knew who was there even before she pushed open the door and peered into the kitchen. "Hello," she said. "This *is* a surprise. Dr. Tompkins said maybe next week."

Tracy smiled at her. "I came in a cab. I still had the key to the apartment. I was going to have everything ready for dinner and surprise you."

Tracy had been making a cake, Ruth noted, an angel food cake. It was just ready for the oven.

"Here, let me," Ruth Ann said, opening the preheated oven and slipping the cake carefully onto the lower rack. "How did you manage? It must have been hard getting from one cupboard to the other, and the angel-food pan is on that high shelf."

142

Tracy grinned. "Let's just say that I managed. I wanted to have everything cleaned up and to be waiting for you with a book in my lap, as if I'd been sitting all afternoon." She looked around at the clutter of bowls and utensils and shook her head. "I'm slow, I guess, but I'll do better with practice."

"You don't have to do better," Ruth Ann assured her. "You don't have to do all this. I'm supposed to be taking care of you."

"No," Tracy said, "we're supposed to be helping each other."

Ruth slipped off her light jacket and reached for the apron hanging inside the broom closet. "What did you do with Mrs. Malcome? When I left this morning, she was muttering about cleaning the refrigerator and washing some curtains."

"I told her she could take the day off," Tracy confessed. "I thought it might be better if we had the evening to ourselves." She watched as Ruth rinsed the dishes and piled them carefully to one side. "I put a couple of potatoes in to bake, and we're having a steak. I picked it up at my favorite market on the way over here."

"It sounds wonderful," Ruth Ann said. "But Tracy, you don't have to worry about these things. All you have to do is take it easy and get to feeling completely well again."

"It was fun," Tracy said. "I was surprised to find

that I could be so . . . so inventive. I used the broom to jiggle the angel-food pan to the edge of the cupboard, and then I tipped it over the edge and caught it as it fell."

Ruth Ann looked at her thoughtfully. "But Tracy, you never eat desserts."

Tracy shrugged. "Oh, I do once in a while. And you like cakes. I remember hearing you say that angel food is your favorite cake."

Ruth Ann peeked through the glass front of the oven. "Well anyway, it looks beautiful." She straightened up and gave Tracy a quick smile. "Now why don't I wheel you into the living room and turn on television? You can watch a couple of shows while I change my clothes and finish getting things ready for dinner."

"If I wanted to watch television," Tracy told her clearly, "I could have watched it in my room at the hospital. If I wanted to be waited on I could have stayed there." She sat up very straight and looked stern. "I thought you were offering me companionship . . . a family. If I had wanted extended hospital service, why would I come here?"

Ruth Ann swallowed. "I just wanted things to be easy for you."

"But I don't want things made easy for me. You said that even if I hadn't been crippled you'd have wanted us to stay together. Didn't you mean it?"

"Of course, I meant it." Ruth Ann turned and looked at her stepmother in the wheelchair. "Tracy, I'm very happy that you're home and I'm sorry if . . . if I've said something to upset you."

Tracy smiled and held out her hand. "I'm happy to be home, too," she said. "And I don't know what we're arguing about. Why don't I start on the salad while you run in and change your clothes? After dinner we can work out a sort of schedule so that we won't be treading on one another's toes."

Ruth went in to change, but it bothered her to know that Tracy was working awkwardly around the kitchen, reaching for things that were out of her way, banging into the stove and the refrigerator, maybe even burning herself. The adjustment would be so much easier for both of them if Tracy would relax.

When Ruth came back to the kitchen, Tracy had the salads ready to go into the refrigerator. The cake wasn't done, but it had raised high above the pan.

"We may as well relax and look at the evening paper for a while," Ruth Ann said, and Tracy nodded.

She switched on the television, almost from force of habit. Mrs. Malcome loved television. But Tracy didn't seem interested in the cartoon show that was on the screen. She wheeled herself across the room to the bookshelf and examined the titles, moving herself slowly along so that she could reach one book and then another.

Ruth watched her for a moment. "Do you like to read, Tracy? I mean do you like to read a lot?"

Tracy turned her head to smile at Ruth. "Yes, I have stacks of books in some of the boxes that came from my place. Could we add them to your collection, do you suppose?"

"Of course," Ruth Ann said. "I suppose these must be some of the heavy boxes Dad had put down in the storeroom. I'll see about having them moved up. Then some evening when there's nothing better to do we can sort them out and stack them."

"Oh, I have this one," Tracy said, taking down a well-worn volume and turning it between her hands. "We'll probably have many duplications."

"Do you like mysteries?" Ruth asked. "Dad loved them, and I guess he passed on the bug to me, but I always prefer the women writers."

They talked about the books until the clock chimed, and Tracy remembered the cake. Ruth ran to rescue it.

Tracy followed her out to the kitchen and got the steak from the refrigerator. "I expect we may as well plan to eat our evening meal early," she said. "That way we won't have all that food in our stomachs at bedtime."

Ruth Ann nodded as she put the inverted cake

pan on a rack and set it aside to cool. "It's tactful of you to say *we,* but you don't have a weight problem. I'm the one who needs the early dinner so I can burn up the extra calories." She looked down at herself and sighed. "I really have lost a little weight, but you'd never know it."

"It takes time," Tracy pointed out. "When you make up your mind seriously to lose weight, you'll have to remember that. You can't expect an overnight miracle."

Ruth looked at her reproachfully. "You sound as if you don't think I *want* to lose weight. You'd never believe how many diets I've gone on these past two years."

"Of course I'd believe it. But they were always crash fad diets that you couldn't possibly stick with, weren't they?"

"I suppose so. Anyway, I didn't stick with any of them. That much is perfectly obvious."

Tracy nodded. "Exactly. But if you'd been on one *reasonable* diet all that time, a diet on which you could lose four or five pounds a month, you'd have lost ... hmmm ... between ninety-six and a hundred and twenty pounds."

"You make it sound easy," Ruth Ann said crossly.

Tracy finished seasoning the steak and turned the oven to broil. She seemed to have dropped the subject of Ruth's weight, but a little later, when they were seated at the table, she brought it up again. "Ruth, can you remember, can you think back and remember whether you weighed more or less than you do now last year at this time?"

Ruth Ann thought back. April, last April, just before the spring formal, the last big dance of the school year. She had started planning right after Christmas. She hadn't mentioned her diet even to Jeanie. If she could manage to take off a pound a week. . . . No, a pound wouldn't be enough; she'd have to take off two or even three pounds. Three pounds would add up to something like thirty-six pounds before the dance. Her father would get her a lovely formal, and even if she didn't have a date she could go stag and everyone would be so *surprised*.

She had made losing weight her resolution for the New Year, writing it in her diary in round firm script. "This year I resolve to lose weight. I'll drink only Diet Cola—no milk shakes or sundaes—and I'll give up pies and cakes and cookies. I'll lose at least two pounds each week until I'm down to the right size, until I can wear a size ten."

Tracy was watching her. Ruth yanked herself back to the present and Tracy's unanswered question. "I weigh almost exactly the same as I weighed a year ago. I have it written down in my diary. I planned to go on a diet after the New Year, and I did . . . for about a week. I figured out that I could lose thirty-six pounds from New Year's Day to the fifth of

148

April. I'd weigh around a hundred and forty then and be able to get into a pretty dress to wear to the spring formal. Only things didn't work out that way. The dress is still in the back of my closet under a plastic bag. Every once in a while I take it out and look at it."

"What dress?" Tracy wanted to know.

Ruth made a little face and helped herself to the salad and sliced beef before answering. "It was stupid, but I really believed that if I got the dress for the prom and had it here as a sort of *promise,* why then I'd have to lose weight. I finally talked Father into it and I bought this yummy dress—a sort of apricot shade in size fourteen. I wanted to get a twelve, but when I told the saleswoman that my sister weighed a hundred and forty pounds, she said I'd better get a fifteen or sixteen. So we compromised and I got a fourteen."

"Tell me more about your sister," Tracy said.

Ruth flushed. "Well, I had to tell her something. She'd have thought I was crazy if I told her I was buying it for my big fat self."

"I think it was a good idea. A psychologically sound idea," Tracy said, and nodded approvingly. "It could have worked, too, if you hadn't been so ambitious. You can see, can't you, that expecting to lose thirty-six pounds in a few weeks was out of the question?"

"Oh, I don't know," Ruth said defensively. "You

read about such things all the time in the newspaper ads."

"Oh those. . . ." Tracy dismissed them with a wave of her hand. "You wouldn't *want* to lose weight that fast. Last year there was a woman in the hospital who had to have an apron of loose skin removed because she lost so much weight so suddenly that her stomach muscles couldn't take care of the loss. Her face looked terrible—all saggy and baggy."

"But when I lose eight or nine pounds, people don't even notice," Ruth Ann pointed out. "I lost eight pounds before your wedding and the only place *I* noticed any difference was in my zipper."

"Of course we noticed," Tracy said gently. "We talked about it one day when we were lying by the pool. Your father said . . . he said that you'd be so much happier when you were free to stop thinking about him, when you had a normal life with dates and boyfriends and all the things you'd missed up till now. I told him you'd really enjoy all those things a lot more, because you'd be older, because they would be new and fresh instead of something you'd had all your life."

"Did you really believe what you were saying?" Ruth asked bluntly. "Or were you trying to make Father feel happier about me?"

"I really meant it. I still mean it." And then she asked a strange question. "Is there a spring formal this year?"

"Yes, in a couple of weeks. I won't be going. I wouldn't go anyway—because of Father—but I especially won't go now."

Tracy looked thoughtful. "But there'll be another formal next spring. You'll be a senior then. You'll go and wear the yummy formal your father gave you and have a wonderful time."

"And live happily ever after, like someone in a fairy tale." Ruth tried to speak lightly, but her throat ached. "I expect next you'll tell me that the boys will be standing in line to take me to the dance."

"I wouldn't say that, but, on the other hand, some oversize girls have a lot of fun. They go on dates and fall in love and eventually get married just like anyone else. But those girls are usually perfectly happy, well-adjusted people. They accept the fact that they're fat and they don't feel sorry for themselves."

"Do you think I feel sorry for myself?" Ruth asked the question in a startled tone and was relieved when Tracy smiled at her.

"Aren't you? A little?"

"Well, a little," she admitted.

"So you see?" Tracy sounded triumphant, as though she had proved her point. "But the majority of fat people hate being fat. They're the ones who wear clothes a size too large in the mistaken hope that they'll *look* thinner; the ones who only weigh themselves early in the morning, who avoid looking in full-length mirrors, and who read everything about diets that they can put their hands on."

"Like me," Ruth said flatly.

"Like all of us, or anyway most of us."

Ruth looked longingly at the last slice of cold steak, and then lifted her eyes to Tracy's face. "Do you really believe I could wear that formal next year?"

"Let's try," Tracy said. "We're going to have to make a great many changes and adjustments this next year. Sometime before the lease on this apartment expires we have to decide on a place to live. You have to decide on whether you'll go to another school or return to this one, and I'll have to work hard at getting out of this blasted chair." There was a grim note in her voice as she concluded. It made Ruth's problem seem hardly a problem at all.

"A year is a long time," Ruth said. "Anything can happen in a year. Let's just plan for a couple of months."

EIGHT

That evening, before she started to get ready for bed, Ruth took the apricot dress from its plastic bag and carried it in to show Tracy. Tracy was already in bed, reading, but she put the book aside when Ruth tapped at the door and looked up with a welcoming smile.

"This is the dress," Ruth said. "Dad was so pleased when I brought it home." She swallowed a little, remembering, and then turned quickly toward the full-length mirror, holding it up before her. "It's a good color for me, don't you think?"

"Very nice," Tracy said. "You'll look beautiful."

Ruth surveyed her mirrored image, then half-closed her eyes so that the reflection blurred and softened into a more flattering picture. She'd wear her hair up, of course, because . . . because . . . it was hard to remember why, and then suddenly she did remember. Her mother had always worn her hair piled high when she dressed for special occasions. Ruth Ann's clearest memory of her mother was of her coming in to kiss Ruth Ann good-night just a few weeks before she became ill. Her parents were going to a formal dinner. Her father wore a dinner jacket and her mother had on a white dress. She had sparkly touches at her throat and in her ears, and her hair sparkled, too, as if it had been dusted with tiny stars. They laughed because she left a rosy imprint on Ruth Ann's cheek when she kissed her. Her mother had looked so lovely and happy that night that the picture was indelibly etched on Ruth Ann's memory.

Abruptly she turned from the mirror and tossed the dress at a nearby chair. "I don't know why I'm kidding myself," she said in a tight harsh voice. "I couldn't look like that in a million years."

Tracy didn't ask what she meant by "like that." She just looked at the dress as it slipped slowly from the chair to a rustling heap on the rug, like a ballet dancer taking a final curtsy.

Ruth Ann picked up the dress and shook it out carefully before draping it over her arm. "Well, I thought you might want to see it," she said. "Good night, Tracy."

"Good night, dear," Tracy said.

Back in her room Ruth didn't even bother putting the dress back into its protective plastic bag. She just put it on a hanger and thrust it in with all the outgrown or seldom-worn articles in her closet. When

154

she returned from school the next day the dress was once again covered and hanging at the back of her closet. She didn't know whether Tracy or Mrs. Malcome had taken care of it.

As Tracy had prophesied the next weeks were filled with change and readjustment, but where once Ruth Ann had clung stubbornly to old and fixed patterns, she found it easier and easier to accept the changes.

First of all there was the problem of what to do about Mrs. Malcome. They didn't really need her, but Ruth Ann hated to be the one to point this fact out, and Tracy didn't seem to feel that it was her place to make the suggestion. In the end Mrs. Malcome, herself, solved the problem. She came in one day, gave the apartment a complete cleaning, and was sitting having a cup of tea with Tracy when Ruth came in from school.

"Oh, hi, Mrs. Malcome," Ruth said. Usually Mrs. Malcome had finished her work and was gone before school was over. She hadn't stayed overnight since Tracy came home from the hospital.

"Why don't you pour yourself a cup of tea and join us?" Tracy said. "Mrs. Malcome and I have been talking."

Ruth Ann got herself a cup and came to the table.

Mrs. Malcome looked at her gravely, and then at Tracy, before she cleared her throat and made her announcement. "It's plain as the nose on your face that you two don't need me any longer," she said ponderously. "Before long you'll be out of school, Ruth Ann, and in the meantime Tracy has taken hold so well that you can manage just fine. I'll be dropping around and keeping an eye on you from time to time, but you don't need the added burden of my salary. So I won't be coming back, except for visits." She took a sip of her tea, and then replaced the cup on the saucer. "Of course, if anything should come up and you *do* need me, you know where to reach me."

"We ... we'll miss you, Mrs. Malcome," Ruth said truthfully. "I'll never forget how kind you've been— not just lately, but all the years you helped take care of Father and me." She spoke carefully so that Mrs. Malcome couldn't possibly suspect the relief she was feeling. "You must promise to come and see us often."

Mrs. Malcome waved this invitation aside, and then sniffed, a sure sign that she was about to be overcome by emotion. "Of course, we'll keep in touch. And when I go to Canada this summer I'll write to you, the same as always. In the meantime, I'll be remembering you in my prayers ... the two of you." She got a handkerchief from her pocket and blew her nose noisily. "Sakes alive," she muttered, "I do believe I'm coming down with one of my spring colds."

Ruth Ann came around the end of the table and gave Mrs. Malcome's plump shoulders a quick squeeze. "You aren't catching a cold at all," she whispered. "You're crying because you hate to leave us just as much as we hate to have you go. But as you say, Tracy and I should get along nicely now, and it isn't as if we're saying good-by forever. We'll probably be screaming for help from time to time."

Mrs. Malcome patted her hand. "You scream whenever you feel like it and you know I'll come running," she said unsteadily. "You're a good girl, Ruthy. You're going to make a fine woman and someday I'll brag that I had some little part in the way you turned out." She turned to Tracy then. "You take good care of her, Mrs. Callahan!"

"I'll try," Tracy said.

They were both a little quiet after Mrs. Malcome was gone, as if they had crossed a bridge that had to be crossed, and then found that it had collapsed behind them when they looked back.

The decision about letting Mrs. Malcome go seemed to tip the scales and start them in another direction. That same evening the landlord came up to talk to them about their lease. He said he realized that they might want to make other arrangements and that he had another tenant interested in the apartment. So if they didn't plan to renew the lease, he would be happy to make an adjustment that would be satisfactory to all concerned.

Tracy said they would talk about it and let him know as soon as they decided. When the man had gone, she asked Ruth to call Mr. Conners to get his opinion on the matter, but a strange voice on the other end of the line reported that Mr. Conners was out of town and not expected back for ten days.

"I guess that leaves it squarely up to us, Ruth. We'll have to decide for ourselves. What do you think we should do?"

"If we're going to move anyway," Ruth Ann said, "I don't suppose a couple of months will make much difference. The only thing is, it might not be too easy to find another place."

"Well, there's always my house," Tracy pointed out. "It isn't rented yet, but, of course, it's quite a distance from your school, if you plan to finish up your senior year there." She made the offer casually, as if she really didn't care one way or another, but Ruth remembered how happy Tracy had been showing her about the little house.

"It wouldn't be too big for us," Ruth said, thinking aloud. "It would be just about the right size. And there aren't any stairs for you to manage. We could probably have a ramp built right up to the patio doors, a removable ramp, of course, so that when you're out of that chair we can have it taken away." She had noticed that Tracy's eyes veered away from hers whenever she talked about the time that Tracy would be able to walk again. Tracy looked away now, but not before Ruth had seen her expression.

"Well, anyway, it's something for us to think about," Tracy said briskly, as if unwilling to pursue the subject. "I've been holding off making a decision about the house until we had a chance to talk about it."

Ruth Ann walked over to the window and looked out. She had been looking at the same view for a long time, for something like eight or nine years. Nothing ever changed except the seasons. It was a well-established neighborhood of solid homes and sturdy apartment buildings. It might be good to have a change, to watch new houses growing up from cement foundations and wooden forms, to see new families settling into the houses, planting trees and lawns and hedges.

"This apartment," she said finally, "is comfortable and convenient and, as you say, it's close to school and to a shopping center and all that, but it's a part of my life that's over. Sometimes I remember. . . . I look around and remember things. I remember that my mother had to stand on a step stool to measure

159

the drapes and that our Christmas tree always stood right there before the window and that there used to be a chandelier over the dining room table. Father kept bumping his head, so they had the fixture shortened. . . ." She paused and looked at Tracy. "You know?"

"Yes, I know."

"So I won't really hate to leave, or anything like that. Once in a while when I hear someone coming along the hall I'm almost sure it's Father, and that in a minute I'll hear his key in the lock and he'll walk in." She stopped then because there was an ache in her throat, but she didn't turn to look at Tracy, because her eyes felt hot and she knew if Tracy offered a word of sympathy she'd probably burst into tears.

Tracy was silent for a long time, and then Ruth Ann heard her wheel the chair across to the kitchen door. When she spoke her voice was perfectly casual. "I think that's probably a very good argument in favor of new surroundings, either the house or another apartment. A wonderful and happy part of your life was spent here, a part of your childhood, but you can't hold on to it forever." And then she went on with determined cheerfulness. "How about a snack before we tune in that late movie? I don't know about you, but I'm starved."

"I'm always starved," Ruth Ann admitted. "I keep telling myself that I'm really not one bit hungry, but my stomach keeps growling back at me."

160

They had a snack. High-protein cereal and non-fat milk. The food didn't exactly satisfy Ruth's hunger, but it was better than nothing, especially when they ate very slowly.

"Tomorrow we weigh in again," Tracy reminded her. "It's been a week."

"I know," Ruth said.

When they had first started the diet, Tracy had suggested that they weigh only once a week. "It's too discouraging when you keep hopping on and off the scales. Your weight can fluctuate as much as two or three pounds during a day, but once a week should give us a good clear picture."

So they weighed on Saturday morning. That first week, fired with enthusiasm, Ruth lost four pounds. The next week she barely managed to keep off the weight she had lost the week before. She cheated a few times, and the transgressions were costly, but Tracy said that she was bound to weaken once in a while.

"Just so you realize that you aren't going to lose weight that way," she said, when Ruth admitted, a little belligerently, that she had stopped and had a milk shake with Jeanie after school.

The milk shake wasn't entirely to blame. The very next day Ruth ate three candy bars, one after another, gobbling them down as though she hadn't eaten for weeks.

"I don't know what was the matter with me," she

161

told Tracy afterward. "The candy machine was sitting there leering at me, and before I knew it I'd put the money into the thing and was eating like a crazy person. I guess I thought that as long as I'd already ruined my diet with the milk shake. . . ."

Tracy nodded. "I know. Why I remember one time—this girl I'm always telling you about. . . ."

"Miss Hypothetical?" Ruth prompted, and they both grinned. Tracy constantly referred to this girl who had faced and conquered all the temptations that beset Ruth.

"Well, *anyway*," Tracy said, "she was going along losing weight and doing her exercises and taking off inches here and there. And then one night she woke up thinking about cream puffs, those fat ones with rich custard fillings and chocolate dribbled all over the top. The trouble was she couldn't *stop* thinking about them; they were an obsession. She told her doctor about it, and he advised her to go to the bakery and buy a cream puff and eat it, and then forget about it. He said it would be better if she just ate *half*, but if she felt she had to she could go ahead and eat it all."

"And did she?" Ruth asked. She didn't really believe in Miss Hypothetical, but she was always fascinated with Tracy's stories about her.

"She bought six," Tracy said sadly. "She bought six and ate every last bite of them. I wish I could

162

tell you that she got sick and has never been able to look a cream puff in the face from that day to this, but I'm afraid she still likes them."

Except for the two or three occasions when Ruth fell from grace, the diet wasn't too hard to follow. Tracy planned most of the meals. She couldn't equal Ruth's cooking, but, as she pointed out, this was probably just as well. Tracy went on the diet with her, although Tracy was supposed to be gaining weight instead of losing it. She managed to eat the same food by having her big meal in the middle of the day and by drinking a large cup of hot chocolate at bedtime.

They had a good breakfast—Tracy insisted on that—and in the early evening they had a substantial dinner, but at luncheon Ruth was on her own. What she ate was a question of morale. If she couldn't resist a hamburger and a side order of French fries, why then she couldn't expect to lose much that week. But if she settled for a salad and rye wafers. . . . It was entirely up to her. Tracy leaned heavily toward hot soups and salads. She said that if you started a meal with a hot soup, so hot that it had to be eaten slowly, it took the edge off one's appetite.

After a few days Ruth grew weary of carrot sticks and celery as hunger appeasers. She learned to do without much salt and actually to enjoy her skim milk, but she hated cottage cheese with a passion. The things she really liked were served in such small portions that she couldn't enjoy them; they were gone too quickly.

Tracy had wanted her to see Dr. Melburn before starting the diet, but Ruth Ann pointed out that she'd just had a checkup. It was required before she could take Physical Education at school, so Tracy compromised by calling Dr. Melburn and talking to him about Ruth.

Jeanie began visiting the apartment again, after Mrs. Malcome left, but the old companionship between the two girls was never resumed. Before long Jeanie had another best friend to share her after-school visits to the malt shop and the Saturday afternoon first-run movies.

One day while Ruth was passing the time, waiting for Tracy to finish a book she was reading, she wandered over to the piano and sat down, letting her fingers run lightly over the keys, seeking out half-remembered chords and melodies. When she looked up, Tracy had closed her book and was watching her.

"Please don't stop," she said, when Ruth noticed her. "All my life I've loved the piano and I've never been able to play a note. Please play something else."

"I wasn't playing anything," Ruth said. "I was just

doodling, but I'll play something if you like." She frowned at the keyboard for a second, trying to decide what to play, and then reached for the book of piano solos, opened a page, and started playing. She played for a long time—almost an hour—and she felt as if an old friend were welcoming her back.

Tracy had wheeled her chair closer, and Ruth could see that she was enjoying the recital. She wasn't trying to make Ruth feel good; she really did enjoy it.

"I used to play a lot," Ruth said, when finally she got up and yawned and stretched. "I was the only one of Mrs. Spencer's students who *wanted* to practice. Only she could never get me in a piano recital. I always had a good excuse for not showing up."

"That's a shame," Tracy said. "Not only for Mrs. Spencer, but for you. It would have been good for you—to be that much better than the others. It's good for anyone to know that he can do one certain thing especially well."

After that Ruth Ann played the piano a lot. She even hunted up some old exercise books and worked with them until her fingers were nimble. It was hard to remember why she had stopped playing. She recalled that one of the times she had gone to Mrs. Spencer's studio for a lesson another pupil had laughed, because Ruth appeared to overflow the piano bench. A small thing, really, and nothing to get the least bit upset about, but Ruth had gone home and cried. Ever since then she hadn't wanted to play the piano, not even when she was by herself.

It was easier to be friendly with the girls at school, some of them were very pleasant, but none of them seemed interested in her. When she told Tracy that, Tracy merely asked, "Are you interested in them?"

"Not really," Ruth admitted. "Maybe that's the trouble with me; I'm just a selfish clod."

Tracy grinned. "You said it. I didn't."

More to show Tracy that she could extend herself to be friendly than because she wanted to pursue the acquaintance, Ruth asked a girl named Carol to come home to listen to a new album. Carol seemed glad to come, and apparently she had a good time. She wouldn't stay for dinner, though, when Tracy and Ruth invited her. She said she had to go home and ride herd on her younger brothers and sisters, because her mother went to work in the evening.

"How many brothers and sisters?" Tracy asked.

Carol made a little face. "Five of them. Ginny, the next oldest, is ten, and they range down to Timmy, who is three. In the middle we have Suzanne and Gary and Joan."

"It must be fun," Ruth said. "I'd love to have brothers and sisters."

166

"They're O.K. some of the time," Carol conceded. "But mostly they're pests. I can't take part in any of the things that go on after school, because I have to be home before six so Mom can get off to work. On Saturdays Dad is home, but he isn't very good with the little ones. They can get away with murder around him."

When Carol left, Ruth walked partway home with her. She did a lot of walking and she didn't seem to get short of breath nearly as much as she had before she started her diet. She might have talked to Carol about the diet, but Carol was on the skinny side. How could you expect her to be anything else after chasing five youngsters day after day.

"Has your mother been in a wheelchair a long time?" Carol asked as they walked, and Ruth told her about the accident. She could speak calmly, almost as if she were telling about something she'd read in the paper.

"Tracy isn't my real mother," Ruth added. "She married my father just a short time before he was killed."

"I thought as much," Carol admitted. "One of the kids at school mentioned something about that. It's nice that you're so fond of one another. I mean, well, you know how some girls are about their stepmothers."

Ruth was pleased without quite knowing why. If

an outsider like Carol noticed that Tracy liked her, it must be true.

"I like your friend," Tracy said, when Ruth came back to the apartment. "We must have her come to see us often."

"Yes, she's nice," Ruth said. Then she added soberly, "It's funny about getting to know people, isn't it? Like reading a new magazine—you see the cover and you have a general idea of what's inside. But still every page can be a surprise."

"I think that's an interesting parallel," Tracy said with a smile.

When they had their Saturday weigh-in, Ruth had lost three more pounds. They weren't going as fast as she'd have liked, but they were going. "At least some of my clothes are getting loose," she told Tracy, "especially around the waist."

"We'll take them in at the seams next week," Tracy said.

Ruth Ann groaned. "You have to be kidding! How can I feel as if I'm losing weight if everything fits like the skin of a banana?"

"We won't have to make them that tight," Tracy comforted her. "This girl I used to know, she found out that taking in clothes helped her a lot. She didn't dare slip into old habits or her clothes wouldn't fit."

"Dear Miss Hypothetical," Ruth murmured. "What would we do without her?"

After they had breakfast, Tracy suggested that they visit the house. "We could take a picnic lunch and go out in a cab and spend most of the day. Would you like that, Ruth? Maybe walking around the place will help us decide whether we want to live there or not."

They spent practically all of the afternoon at the little house. Ruth found an old length of hose in the new garage, and while they attempted to water the lawn a neighbor came over and offered to loan them her garden hose and sprinkler. She was a nice grandmotherly-looking woman, who introduced herself as Mrs. Durham. "I'm so glad that someone will be living here," she told Tracy earnestly. "We understood that the house wasn't for sale. Some people have stopped and asked us about it, so I called and asked the real-estate man."

"I expect we were trying to make up our minds," Tracy said.

"Oh." Mrs. Durham looked blank for a moment. "Well, anyway, it'll be nice to have neighbors. Are there just the three of you?"

"Just the two of us, I'm afraid. My husband died some time ago." Tracy didn't explain that Ruth was only her stepdaughter, although Ruth was subconsciously braced for it.

"Ah, that's a pity," Mrs. Durham said sympathetically. "But you'll enjoy the neighborhood—quite a

169

few young people." She looked at Ruth again. "I expect you go to school, yet."

"Yes, I'll be a senior next year," Ruth told her.

"My girls will be glad about that. Kathleen's about your age, and Theresa's a year and a half younger. I have a son, too. He's away in the Air Force right now, but he'll be home soon after Christmas. He'll be very interested in knowing that a pretty girl is living next door." She chattered for a while longer, and then remembered that her clothes were ready to go in the dryer, so she had Ruth come over and get the hose and sprinkler.

"Don't bother about bringing them back," she told Ruth. "I'll have Charlie pick them up later."

Ruth returned to Tracy, and when they had the sprinkler going, they went into the house and planned where they were going to place the furniture. Without even having to say the words, they had decided to move into the little house. Mentally they hung the curtains and placed each stick of furniture.

"We won't have to buy anything but the rugs," Tracy said once. And then a little later she added, "And a washer and dryer. We'll almost have to have those unless we want to run back and forth to a laundromat. Of course, that might not be too bad." She broke off and chewed her lip for a moment before going on. "Ruth, do you suppose you could learn to drive the car? It would make things so much simpler. We wouldn't have to worry about your getting back and forth to school next year if you drove."

Ruth Ann took a deep breath. "Do you mean it? You'd let me learn to drive your car?"

"Our car," Tracy said. "And yes, of course, I mean it. I'd hate to sell it. I couldn't possibly get back the money I've invested in it, and it may be months before I'll be able to drive again."

"I've always wanted to learn to drive, but Dad said it was foolish, because I'd never have the car since he drove it to work. I even took the course at school and I got a good grade in it."

"We'll sign you up with a good driving school," Tracy said. "There must be dozens of them. And, of course, we'll have to make some changes in the insurance policy." She noticed that Ruth was grinning. "Now what?" she asked.

"I was thinking about Jeanie. She's had her learner's permit for almost a year, but her mother tries to teach her and then her father tries and they all start yelling at one another."

"I can believe it," Tracy said. "No, the driving school is a much better idea. Maybe we can call someone tonight."

They had their picnic lunch, and then moved the sprinkler around to the back of the house. "We'll have to get a birdbath," Ruth said dreamily. "One of those pedestal affairs. It's so much fun to watch the birds splashing around."

"But not quite so much fun cleaning up after them," Tracy reminded her.

They could scarcely believe it when the cab came back to pick them up. The hours had simply flown.

"We ought to be able to move in a week," Tracy said, as both of them turned to look back at the house. "We'll find out about having the telephone connected and getting a moving van."

"And about the driving lessons," Ruth reminded her.

"You'll probably pick it up in no time," Tracy said.

Ruth Ann settled back in her corner of the cab and thought about driving to school in Tracy's beautiful car. She could see it all, like a sequence unfolded on a movie screen. The surprised looks and the questions and the admiration. She could see herself getting out of the car, rolling up the windows, and checking the doors. Only the girl she imagined was much slimmer than the Ruth who was doing the dreaming. Someone would ask if the car was hers. She would explain, casually, of course, that it had belonged to Tracy, but since Tracy couldn't drive for a while she had insisted that Ruth use it.

NINE

It hardly seemed possible that things could move ahead so fast.

On Monday Ruth took her first driving lesson, and she was so excited that she forgot all about being shy and awkward with the pleasant young man who was her instructor. He was a homely, matter-of-fact young fellow, who said, even after that first lesson, that Ruth was going to make an excellent driver. "I'm glad you're not the excitable type," he told her. "I get a lot of those."

He gave her a manual to study and made an appointment for the following day. "In a week we'll have you buzzing around like Barney Oldfield," he told her, as he let her off in front of the apartment building.

"Who's Barney Oldfield?" Ruth asked Tracy, when she got back to the apartment, and Tracy said she wasn't sure . . . some kind of racing driver, she thought.

The second and third lessons went as well as the

173

first. Ruth read her driver's manual faithfully, but she could still hardly believe it when the instructor said, after the fourth lesson, that she was ready for her test. "Don't worry about it, and above all don't get flustered," he advised her. "You'll do fine."

During that week Ruth was so busy with school, her driving lessons, and helping Tracy sort and pack the things for moving that she almost forgot about being hungry. Eating was just a habit anyway, she told herself. If you keep busy and interested you don't have to eat all the time.

At the next Saturday weigh-in she found that she had lost another five pounds. Tracy fussed over her. She said that it wasn't good to lose weight quite that fast, but, of course, Ruth was delighted.

All the arrangements were made for the move. The van would be at the apartment on Wednesday afternoon. Everything would be packed when Ruth returned from school. On Monday she would take her driver's test. If she passed. . . . But of course she would pass! She felt perfectly at home behind the wheel of the car.

Over the weekend she and Tracy kept remembering things they might forget and writing notes. Little pieces of paper were pinned all along the kitchen curtains. "Have telephone connected on Wednesday." "Cancel paper and reorder for new address." "Put in a change-of-address card."

Sunday evening Mrs. Malcome dropped in to see

174

them, and the first thing she said was, "Ruth Ann, what have you been doing to yourself? You've lost so much weight!"

Ruth Ann hugged her. "Mrs. Malcome, that's the nicest thing you've ever said to me."

Mrs. Malcome was glad they were moving into Tracy's house. She assured them that time was the great healer and that they would find more and more comfort in being together. "It does my heart good," she told them solemnly, "to see the way you look out for one another. Mr. Callahan, God rest him, couldn't have left a better estate to either of you. A daughter for Tracy to see her through all trouble and worry, and a mother to look after you, Ruth. It's almost like the story of Ruth in the Bible."

Ruth didn't dare ask what she meant by that last remark. She knew Mrs. Malcome well enough to know that once you got her started she could go on and on and on.

Tracy changed the subject skillfully by asking Mrs. Malcome's opinion about packing something. When Mrs. Malcome had gone, Tracy looked across the room at Ruth and smiled. "She's really a very nice person, Ruth. And she's devoted to you."

"I know. Mrs. Malcome's O.K., but she does get pretty sticky at times."

Tracy nodded in agreement. "Yes, she does."

"But it was nice of her to notice I'd lost weight," Ruth continued happily. "I didn't think it was even *noticeable.*" She walked over to the mirror and turned her head this way and that. "Those exercises must be doing some good, though, I seem to be missing at least one chin."

"As soon as we're moved and settled," Tracy said, "we'll get right to work on taking in your clothes. You'll be surprised how many people will notice then."

On Monday Ruth passed her driving test with ease. She got her temporary license and brought it home to show Tracy. "Look at it," she said. "It's as beautiful as a check for a million dollars."

"Maybe it is," Tracy said. "I've never seen a check for a million dollars."

Jeanie didn't try to hide her envy. "Some people have all the luck," she muttered, as she walked to the library with Ruth to return some books. "I'll probably never pass my test. Dad thinks that driving schools are a waste of time and money, but he and Mother yell at me so much that I can't keep my mind on what I'm doing."

"Tracy says that people should never try to learn from members of their own family," Ruth said, and Jeanie scowled at her.

"Ruth Ann, I don't suppose you realize, but you start almost every sentence that way."

"What way?"

"*Tracy says.* It's Tracy says this and Tracy says

that. Tracy says you should forget about salt when you're on a diet. Tracy says that vitamin pills aren't really necessary when people eat the right foods. Tracy says that insurance is an investment in the future. I'm getting sick of hearing what Tracy says!"

"I'm sorry," Ruth Ann said. "I didn't know I was being such a bore."

"Well, you are," Jeanie snapped. "My goodness, you aren't a bit of fun these days. All of a sudden everything is so serious. You only talk about the future. A sixteen-year-old girl isn't supposed to be thinking about things so far ahead."

"I guess that depends on what sixteen-year-old girl you're talking about," Ruth said slowly. "When my father was here to look after me and make the decisions, I thought about the future as something far away and not too important. But now I have to look ahead and make plans. Someone has to do it, and it wouldn't be fair to dump all the responsibility on Tracy's shoulders."

"I don't see why not," Jeanie countered. "She's an adult and she's supposed to worry about things. Anyway, my mother says that Tracy didn't do so badly for herself."

They went into the library and exchanged some books for Jeanie. Ruth Ann went around and said good-by to all her favorite librarians, because in the new neighborhood she'd be visiting a new library.

Mrs. Stacy, who had been her friend for a long

time, said she'd miss her and told Ruth to be sure to drop in for a visit whenever she came by. She asked for Ruth's new address, and then said brightly, "Oh, you'll be going to the North Woodland branch. Miss Lupin is the new librarian there. You'll like her, Ruth Ann. She's a charming person."

"Do you know *all* the librarians?" Ruth asked.

Mrs. Stacy smiled and nodded. "Just about all of them, at least in this county. It's as if we belong to a big club."

"Do you have to be terribly smart to be a librarian, Mrs. Stacy? The reason I ask . . . well, next year I'll be a senior, and I think it's time I thought about what I'm going to *be*."

Mrs. Stacy smiled at her. "Why not find out if you really like it first? Join the library staff at your school. Mrs. Phillips is an excellent teacher, and she's always crying for new helpers."

"I thought about it once last year," Ruth Ann admitted. "But I've always hated to join things because I'm so big."

Mrs. Stacy nodded, as if this remark made perfectly good sense. She was a large woman, and she probably knew exactly what Ruth Ann was talking about. "Well, anyway, you think about it," she said.

When the two girls were walking home, Ruth Ann remembered what Jeanie had said about Tracy and returned to the subject. "What does your mother mean when she says that Tracy didn't do so badly for herself?"

Jeanie shrugged. "Well, everyone knows that your father left her all that money and property and insurance, and now that she's your guardian she has control of everything your father left *you*. She's a well-to-do widow, and she's young enough so that she probably won't have any trouble getting married again. Even being in the wheelchair isn't too bad, because my father says the insurance man told him that Tracy had some fabulous accident and disability insurance. No, Tracy didn't do so badly."

For a moment Ruth Ann was so mad that she couldn't speak. She kept seeing Tracy's face. How lovely she had looked on her wedding day, and the tears in her eyes when Ruth had given her the gift. She remembered the pain that was always in Tracy's eyes now, even when she smiled, and the shadows that sometimes touched her face.

She looked at Jeanie thoughtfully for a long moment, and then she smiled. How could she get mad at anyone as alarmingly stupid as Jeanie? She could only be sorry for her.

"Good-by, Jeanie," Ruth said, when they got back to the apartment.

Jeanie looked offended. "Aren't you going to ask me to come in?"

Ruth shook her head. "No." Then she leaned closer and spoke in a dramatic whisper, "You see, I

179

have to help Tracy count her gold and silver pieces. She's storing them in a big trunk, to avoid taxes, you know. When we get to the new house we'll go out some dark night and bury them in the yard."

Jeanie looked annoyed. "I think you're crazy," she said flatly.

Mr. Conners came back to town and called to find out how Tracy and Ruth were getting along. He was astonished to hear what had been going on during his absence, but Ruth could tell by his voice that he was pleased, too. He said that he and Mrs. Conners were inviting themselves over for a visit, just as soon as she and Tracy were settled, but in the meantime if they needed a chauffeur. . . .

"Oh, we have a chauffeur," Ruth told him. "I've been taking driving lessons, and just yesterday I passed my test. Tracy called the man about fixing up the insurance and it's all settled. They put me on her policy. I'll be driving back and forth to school until the semester's over."

Mr. Conners talked to Tracy then, and she told him about the arrangements they had made for the lease. It was nice to know that Mr. Conners was pleased with them, just as it was nice to know that he was always there, ready with advice if they ever should need it.

The landlord brought up the boxes from the basement storeroom, so that all their belongings would be together when the movers came. Tracy opened one of the cardboard cartons and pulled out a photograph album and a slim leather-bound book. "Come here, Ruth. I want you to see these. I know you haven't really believed me—about Miss Hypothetical."

Ruth Ann came over to look across Tracy's shoulder. "You mean there really is such a person? You have pictures of her?" She picked up the leather volume. "This is a school yearbook, isn't it?" She flipped open a few pages at random, and then handed the book back to Tracy. "All right," she said challengingly, "show me your Miss Hypothetical."

Tracy opened the book and turned the pages slowly. Finally she stopped and pointed at a group picture. "There . . . on the left in the back row."

Ruth Ann squinted. "You can't tell what she looks like from that. She could be just about any fat girl. She could be *me* even. Don't you have any better pictures of her?"

"I think so." Tracy opened the photograph album and started turning the pages rapidly. "Here's one taken when she was eight or nine. She was a little chubby even then. And this one was taken the year she started high school. Here she's eighteen. Wasn't she enormous?"

Ruth Ann looked at the picture of the fat girl and a fat older woman. She was nagged by a feeling of recognition. "Who's the other one? The older woman?" she asked finally.

181

Tracy sighed. "That's my mother. She was ill, even then, although you'd never guess it."

"*Your* mother?" Ruth stared at Tracy, and then looked back at the picture. "But that means. . . ."

"That's right," Tracy said mildly. "*I* was Miss Hypothetical."

"I can't believe it," Ruth Ann said, stunned. She looked closer, and then shook her head. "I mean, I just took it for granted that you'd always been thin."

Tracy made a little face. "At the time my mother died," she said, "I weighed over two hundred pounds."

Ruth was still examining the photograph. The features resembled Tracy's, but she looked so different. Why she looked older in the long-ago picture than she looked today! "How long," she heard herself asking, "how long did it take you to lose that much weight?"

"Not long. After I'd once made up my mind that it had to be done. I guess that's always the hardest part. Making up one's mind. When I first went into nurses' training I had to buy special uniforms. The regular ones wouldn't fit. Most of the department heads were pretty blunt about the way I looked. I don't know why, but I had the idea that in nursing it wouldn't matter that I was heavy and awkward. I guess I saw myself as a king-size Florence Nightin-

182

gale. But I soon found out that there were as many slim attractive girls in nurses' training as anywhere else."

Ruth Ann nodded. Tracy didn't have to explain any further. "Was it hard?" she asked.

"Losing the weight? You'd better believe it was hard! Sometimes I told myself that it was impossible. I'd let it pile up for such a long time, you see. Overeating was more than a bad habit; it was a way of life. But there's one good thing about nurses' training, you don't have time to sit around and feel sorry for yourself. And I had a friend, a very good friend. One of the nurses in charge of our training program took an interest in me. Or maybe she was sorry for me. At any rate, she helped me and encouraged me. Sometimes I almost hated her. She used to order my meals and I'd look around at the other girls eating creamed chicken while I nibbled a salad, and I'd tell myself it wasn't *worth* it."

Tracy turned to the last page of the album and pointed to a snapshot. "Miss Gilham took this picture when I was just getting started on the diet." She pointed to another snapshot. "This one was taken a little better than a year and sixty-five pounds later."

The second snapshot was one of Tracy proudly wearing a trim uniform and her nurses' cap.

Ruth Ann sat down on the arm of a chair and smiled at Tracy, hugging the class yearbook up close to her chest. "But Tracy, why didn't you tell me all this before?"

"Tell you what? That I'd managed to lick the weight problem, and so could you? Do you really think that would have made you feel more friendly toward me?"

"No, I guess not," Ruth said. "But why are you telling me now?"

"Because you've already decided to lose the weight. You already *know* that come next spring you'll be able to wear your beautiful dress and be the belle of the ball."

Ruth was studying the picture again. "It still doesn't seem possible that you ever looked like this. These photographs are like those ads in the paper you're always scoffing about."

"Not quite like that," Tracy said firmly. "I lost my weight over a period of months instead of weeks, and I should hesitate to tell you this, but there were several periods when I lost scarcely any weight at all. I'd get discouraged and go on an eating binge, but then Miss Gilham would give me a pep talk, and I'd go back on my diet again." She sighed, remembering, and then she smiled. "Poor Miss Hypothetical, she really did have a struggle, but finally there came the day when she was hurrying across the street from the nurses' home to the hospital and some young boys in a car whistled at her."

"Did they really? And you liked it? You weren't mad or anything?"

"Mad? I was delighted! Then a few weeks after that one of the nurses asked me to go on a blind date with her. The girls did that a lot, but they'd never asked me before."

"Did you go?"

"Not that time," Tracy said. "But afterward I started going out once in a while. I always had such a good time that the young men asked me to go out with them again. It was all so new to me, you see, and they liked that. I wasn't bored with everything. Interns don't have much money—sometimes we even went Dutch treat—but I enjoyed a second-run movie and a bag of popcorn, no butter of course." She took the book from Ruth and tucked it back into the carton with the photograph album. "Now," she said briskly, "now that I've told you my guilty secret I suppose we might as well get at the rest of the sorting. You do have to go to school tomorrow."

Ruth thought about their conversation that night when she was in bed waiting for sleep to come. Seeing the pictures of Tracy made her know, more than ever, that she really could lose weight, even though it wouldn't be an overnight miracle.

And their conversation made her understand so many things that had puzzled her about Tracy. It even explained the night at the hospital when Tracy had looked at her with the eyes of a stranger and called her *me* and begged her to go away. The heavy sedation and pain, of course, were the main reasons, but also Tracy was remembering the pain and frustration of being a misfit. She was seeing it all start again with Ruth.

All the years Tracy had lived with her mother and taken care of her, Tracy had been overweight. It hadn't mattered only because she hadn't let it matter. But when she was alone and looking around for a direction to her life—

Like me, Ruth thought, *like me.*

Tracy had been older, but she had probably been just as frightened as Ruth of not having anyone to belong to and care about. But she had found a friend.

She remembered how Tracy had been so apologetic about her lovely clothes. "There were so many years when I couldn't wear them," she had said. And then later she had told Ruth that she couldn't let her use *her* as an excuse for pushing life away.

Ruth fell asleep at last, and she dreamed that she was the one in the wheelchair, with Tracy looking after *her*. Only it wasn't an upsetting dream, not a bit like a nightmare.

"What shall we do with this?" Tracy asked the next day, when Ruth rushed in from school to help with the last-minute items.

The movers had almost emptied the apartment, but there were still some precious things that they would transport in the car. Lamps, photographs, and the beautiful bottle of brandy, which Tracy was holding in her hands.

Ruth took it and turned it so that the light caught the glass and sparkled like diamonds. "It's like an old friend," she said. "I remember when Dad brought it into the apartment and put it up on the mantel when they came back from their Mexican holiday. It's always been like a promise, a promise of something wonderful that's going to happen, something so wonderful that it would be an excuse for opening the bottle. We'll have to save it for a very special occasion."

"For the time when you can zip yourself into that dress," Tracy said.

"Oh no, it has to be more special than that. Maybe, maybe the day you get out of that chair, when you can run up and down stairs like you used to."

"We won't pack it," Tracy said. "I'll carry it on my lap."

Ruth handed the bottle to her. "Yes," she said. "You do that."

Whether they opened the bottle or not didn't really matter, she thought with startling clarity. It would probably be better if they never opened it. If the occasion never seemed quite important enough, the bottle would always be there. They would always have a promise of better times to come.

The men came to move the piano. It would be the last thing to go into the van. Ruth went down to watch them, and she found that quite a few people had stopped to watch the movers as they trundled the heavy piano onto a cart and then up a narrow ramp into the bed of the truck.

"Hey, Ruth Ann, are you the one who's moving?" She turned her head and saw Tony Barretto. He had his motor scooter propped up against the building, and he was watching the men juggle the furniture and crates into place.

"Yes, we're moving to Bellevue."

"Before school's out?"

"Oh, I'll be driving back and forth," she told him. "I'll probably be back for my senior year, too. It really isn't far when you drive."

"Will you be going to the spring formal?" he asked, and she remembered at once that Tony was head of the dance committee. Naturally he'd want everyone to be there.

"I don't think so," she said, and Tony looked embarrassed.

"No, of course, you wouldn't be going . . . because of your father. But next year will be different, hey?"

"Yes, next year will be different."

"So maybe next year you'll save me a dance," he said, and it was hard to tell if he was kidding or really meant what he said. He probably did mean it, Tony was such a nice friendly boy, and by next spring he'd probably have forgotten all about it. But she couldn't help hoping that he would remember.

"Yes," she said, "I'll be happy to save you a dance."

She watched Tony as he got back on his motor scooter and roared off around a corner. He'd probably be scared to death if he knew how much she had daydreamed about him these past months. It never seemed to bother Tony that she was fat and awkward and didn't have a line of chatter. Tony liked everyone. He probably hadn't even noticed that she was losing weight. But when school started next fall he'd have to notice. She could imagine the way his brown eyes would widen. She could hear him call her, "Ruth Ann?" he'd say. "But it can't be. . . ."

Ruth was smiling as she went up to tell Tracy that the movers had gone and would be waiting for them at the house.

They looked around the apartment for the last time, and then went down to get into the car that Ruth had parked at the rear of the apartment building. Tracy got into the car much more easily now, but whether because she was getting used to her

189

handicap or because her leg muscles were really responding was hard to tell.

Ruth folded the wheelchair and slipped it into the back seat. She got in behind the wheel then, and turned her head to smile at Tracy. "Are we ready?"

"Yes," Tracy said. "Let's go home."

Home. . . . It had a nice sound.

She started the car and turned out into the traffic, as if she'd been driving all her life. Her eyes were on the road ahead, but her thoughts were miles beyond the turning wheels. A new life and a new home, and the promise of all the tomorrows that would unfold before her.

ZOA SHERBURNE lives in Seattle, Washington. At present the household consists of a mother-in-law, four of her eight children, and three parakeets. A son in the Air Force, three married daughters, two grandsons, and twin granddaughters complete the family.

"When we are all together," she says, "the neighbors insist that they can see the walls inhale and exhale. It must prove that a writer can write under any conditions."

Mrs. Sherburne's first novel for girls, ALMOST APRIL, was published in 1956. Since then she has written eight others. She has also written stories for a great variety of magazines.